Please return/renew this item by the last date shown on this label, or on your self-service receipt.

To renew this item, visit **www.librarieswest.org.uk** or contact your library

Your borrower number and PIN are required.

Libraries**West**

Unable to sit still without reading, **Bella Frances** first found romantic fiction at the age of twelve, in between deadly dull knitting patterns and recipes in the pages of her grandmother's magazines. An obsession was born! But it wasn't until one long, hot summer, after completing her first degree in English Literature, that she fell upon the legends that are Mills & Boon books. She has occasionally lifted her head out of them since to do a range of jobs, including barmaid, financial adviser and teacher, as well as to practise (but never perfect) the art of motherhood on two (almost grown-up) cherubs.

Bella lives a very energetic life in the UK, but tries desperately to travel for pleasure at least once a month—strictly in the interests of research!

Books by Bella Frances

Mills & Boon Modern Romance

The Playboy of Argentina

Claimed by a Billionaire

The Argentinian's Virgin Conquest
The Italian's Vengeful Seduction

Mills & Boon Modern Tempted

The Scandal Behind the Wedding
Dressed to Thrill

Visit the Author Profile page
at millsandboon.co.uk for more titles.

THE CONSEQUENCE
SHE CANNOT DENY

BY
BELLA FRANCES

MILLS & BOON

First Published in Great Britain 2017
By Mills & Boon, an imprint of HarperCollins*Publishers*
1 London Bridge Street, London, SE1 9GF

© 2017 Bella Frances

ISBN: 978-0-263-93401-4

Our policy is to use papers that are natural, renewable and recyclable products and made from wood grown in sustainable forests. The logging and manufacturing processes conform to the legal environmental regulations of the country of origin.

Printed and bound in Spain
by CPI, Barcelona

THE CONSEQUENCE
SHE CANNOT DENY

For Dad

Whose moral compass is always due north

Thank you for always being there
At my back but pointing forwards
Helping me on my way

CHAPTER ONE

Heavenly things are about to happen!

SO DECLARED THE press pack for *Heavenly* magazine, in an elegant cursive font across its front cover.

I'm absolutely sure they are, thought Coral Dahl as she sat back on the cream leather of Romano Publishing's executive jet and started flicking through the folder. *Fingers crossed they'll happen to me...*

Heavenly's tagline summed up how *she* was feeling about this trip, but for the posse of fashion, art and creative directors, stylists, hair and make-up assistants and editorial staff it was just another day at the office. Celebrity fashion editorials were no big deal to them, but for Coral, as a rookie photographer, it was the biggest career step of her life.

In less than an hour they would be landing on Hydros, the infamous private island belonging to the infamously private Di Visconti family. They'd spend the next two days photographing the heir apparent, Salvatore, and his fiancée before their ultra-hush-hush, ultra-exclusive wedding. All after signing confidentiality agreements. In triplicate.

'OK, people, listen up.' Mariella, the senior editor, walked through the cabin, looking more than a little flustered. 'Word is that Salvatore's brother Raffaele, our very own commander-in-chief, is going to be there, overseeing things. Yes, I hear you gasp, but I don't want anyone in a panic or fluttering too many eyelashes—I'll handle everything. We're professionals, and we all know what we're doing. Well, nearly all of us,' she added, looking at Coral. 'So there shouldn't be any problems. Just let me reassure him. We go way back, and whatever it is that's got him ruffled I'll sort it out.'

Coral looked around. Everyone seemed to be grabbing their bags and reapplying their make-up.

'What's going on?' she asked the girl next to her.

'Raffaele Rossini—CEO of Romano. Signor Smokin' Hot!' She laughed, slicking her lips with gloss. 'None of us stands a chance, but it doesn't stop us from trying.'

Coral raised her eyebrows. She wouldn't be trying anything with anyone. This trip was strictly business. She'd only vaguely heard of the Di Visconti family before she'd been handed her brief, two hours earlier, but now she knew plenty about the late Giancarlo, founder of the billion-dollar Argento Cruise Line, and his son Salvatore. And, of course, the more mysterious Raffaele Rossini, head of the entire Romano Publishing empire, which just happened to publish *Heavenly*—the magazine for which she'd won this commission.

'Nobody gets close to Raffaele. He's like a god, up in the clouds, so it's really amazing that we're going to meet him.'

Coral flicked back through the pages of the press pack, past images from the nineteen-fifties of the first cruise liner in the Argento fleet right up to recent shots of their twelve amazing vessels. It was the most exclusive cruise line in the world. She scanned them for information about Raffaele, but all she could see was that he had an architect-designed cliffside house along the coast from the family's ancient villa, and that he had launched a bunch of magazines over the years. Oh, and his net worth was billions.

'It hardly says anything in the press pack about Raffaele,' she said, frowning.

'Yes, that's how he likes it,' said Mariella, bustling up. 'Trust me—the fact that he's getting personally involved is not something that happens every day. So, top of your game everyone. Coral, are you well prepared? It's a tiny little shoot with Kyla this afternoon. We'll do it outside— on the loggia. Yes? Happy with that? No need for any fancy ideas, OK, sweetie? Try not to panic. Speak only if spoken to. Leave it to the pros.'

Coral's heart sank. Outdoors? The loggia? So her creative input was going to be limited as to where to position the reflective umbrella. After all the effort she had put in to winning this commission.

Her portfolio had been super-sharp, super-artistic. She could just imagine her mother gasping when she heard about this. Lynda Dahl would be horrified to hear that the pinnacle of her talented daughter's art school career was a point-and-click camera shoot with some billionaire's babe.

Oh, well. It was a start. The start she and her mother had dreamed of for years. And it was on Hydros. *And* she'd be published in *Heavenly*. All things considered, that was pretty good going for her first month as a professional photographer.

Despite the air-conditioned chill, Coral warmed at the thought of her mother. After everything she had been through, the pride on her mum's face when she'd watched Coral graduate had been the best feeling ever. Even though this job wasn't high art, Coral knew that it was going to mean the world to Lynda.

Inside, the team were getting more and more hyper, but outside the Adriatic Sea was calm and jewel-blue. The jet's wing sparkled in the sunshine. The whole day twinkled like a golden blessing. This was going to be the start of an amazing chapter in her life. She could feel it. Things were finally turning around…

The plane landed smoothly, the wait to disembark was mere moments, and then they stepped out into the spectacular sunshine of the Adriatic springtime.

She walked away from the magazine staff and tried to call Lynda. The confidentiality clause was real, but her mother was a worrier. And when she worried she got anxious, and when she got anxious…

That was something to be avoided at all costs.

There was no answer. Out of the corner of her eye Coral saw them all skipping off towards some cars.

She sent a text.

Touched down on a secret island in Greece! On my way to meet the client! Wish I could tell you more but I'm sworn to secrecy! Hugs xx

That should do it, she thought, tucking the phone back into her bag and running to catch up to where the others were all standing like a chorus line, bubbling with excitement. She came up right up behind them—and then saw what had their attention.

There, in between shoulders, she glimpsed a fleet of cars. They were parked one behind the other. The drivers' doors were open and standing at each one was a man in black trousers and shirt. Everyone seemed to be staring, waiting.

And then, from one of the cars, a man emerged.

'Oh, my God,' she heard being whispered along the row. *'Everybody take cover. Here comes the walking sex bomb.'*

Coral strained to see clearly. Was Raffaele Rossini

really such a big deal? With her photographer's eye she scanned and judged.

Tall and toned—just like they all were. Proportions? Perfect. Head to shoulder, chest, waist, hips, legs. Handsome? Yes. Off the charts. Brown hair as opposed to black. Shorter than execs normally wore it. And a close-cropped beard that sculpted his cheeks, lips and jaw. Stubble wasn't her thing. Normally.

He moved around the cars and then she felt it. *Wow.* There was no way to deny that this man was utterly magnetic.

But he was going to be her boss. Off-limits was the only rule that applied.

He moved forward slowly. There was nothing to see under the mirrored shades of his Aviators. The slant of his mouth was neutral. But the slow nod of his head as he checked them all out was like a caress. His voice, when he spoke, an embrace. They sighed as they budged a little closer.

'Welcome to the Island of Hydros. I hope you had a good flight. My men will escort you to your villas and make sure you're comfortable.'

Mariella breathed her appreciation as everyone else fluttered *thank you* with their eyelashes.

'You have all signed non-disclosure agreements, so you're fully aware that there will be no unauthorised photography, recording or social media.'

The gang gushed an obedient yes. He turned to Mariella.

'And your protégée, Mariella—where is she?'

As if she was infected with some plague, everyone shuffled away from Coral. The dust from the ground swirled and the wind blew her hair. Coral lifted her hand to sweep it from her face as his gaze zoomed to her.

'This is Coral Dahl, Raffa. She's the one I told you about.'

Coral smiled and waited for him to speak, but he didn't. His eyes flashed over her quickly, and then he seemed to nod slightly.

'You won the commission to photograph Kyla.'

It didn't sound like a question, but she found herself nodding.

'Yes, that's right. I'm really thrilled to meet you and get a chance to work on the magazine.'

He stared.

Silence settled over the whole group as he began to walk towards her.

'Let's talk about that as we drive. Pass me your bag.'

She looked down stupidly to the huge leather tote that doubled as handbag, briefcase and holdall.

'No, no. It's fine. I'll manage,' she said cheerfully.

He waited, as if she hadn't understood him, and then she got it. Obviously whatever Raffaele said, happened. No questions, no rebuttals, no argument. She handed it to him. *Fine.*

'There.' He indicated the second car in the line—low and sleek, compared to the four-wheel drives. He opened the passenger door and she slid inside.

She scented leather and musk, and then the man who got in beside her. The brilliant day was left behind as he closed the door and sealed them in.

She didn't so much as glance to the side as they passed the others but she could sense them all staring. Raffaele turned off down a narrow road and immediately put his foot down. She lurched back, grabbed at the seatbelt.

'So, Coral, tell me a little bit about yourself.'

'Well, I'm twenty-four. I live in London, in a little flat in Islington. I work in a café round the corner. But all my life I've wanted to be a fashion photographer. So that's why this commission is my dream come true.'

'I see. And you studied art?'

She braced herself as he took the corners on the road which twisted like a corkscrew along the cliff.

'Yes, I started out doing Fine Art. My mother is an artist and I practically lived in art galleries growing up. She took me all over the country when she could. When she wasn't...'

'Wasn't?'

'What I mean is, I chose photography for my Master's because my mother had struggled so hard to make ends meet. I want to have a creative career but with an income, and—'

'It's a crowded market. What makes you think you will succeed?'

'Because I'm good,' she said. She didn't mean it as a boast. She knew she was good.

She waited to see what he was going to say, but he drove on in silence. From the corner of her eye she could see the length of his thigh and the hard muscle that flexed as he pressed on the pedals. There was no doubt about his physical perfection, but it was almost impossible to read what he was thinking.

'You took a Master's in photography. And my senior creative director thought your work was outstanding.'

'Thanks,' she said, suddenly brightening. Finally a compliment.

'But, for me, this is too important a project to take risks with a novice.'

So that was what the problem was. Oh, dear. It wasn't all going to land in her lap after all.

'Let's start with the creative angle. What have you got in mind? A story? A concept?'

So much for outdoors on the loggia. *She* wasn't going to be the one to tell him that Mariella had it all decided. Her heart raced. Her mind ran. She looked at the vista, the distant scattering of volcanic islands wrapped in ribbons of blue sun and sea.

'Of course! I—I've been thinking since we took off— knowing that the light would be so good and the colours so strong—that I'd like to take a fresh look at the Greek goddess trope.'

Words poured from her mouth before she even knew what they were, but it was obvious that she had to sell him something pretty amazing or she was going to be sent home.

'When I think of Athena and all those mythical goddesses I'm seeing seventies women—liberated, but still incredibly feminine. I want to use the clarity of the landscape and the light and juxtapose it with soft silhouettes.'

'I see.' He frowned as he turned down a road.

A modern building came into view, its huge windows curving off to the right as it hugged the cliff.

He parked and got out beside a wide stone entrance where two huge black dogs lay sleeping in the sun. She glanced up at him as she got out of the car. His eyes were still hidden behind sunglasses, his mouth impassive. But at least he wasn't telling her to go home.

'Avanti,' he said.

He touched her arm lightly, swung her bag over his shoulder and guided her to the wide steps. The dogs watched carefully as she passed, but didn't make a move.

Inside, light beamed down—radiant and golden. Every single surface reflected understated wealth, from the crystal glints of an elegant chandelier to the aquamarine depths of a sunken rock pool that stopped her dead in her tracks.

'Wow!' she said, unable to hide her awe.

'Aphrodite's Pool,' he said. 'It is said that she bathed the baby Adonis in it.'

Coral wandered closer. The water babbled like giggling children. But beneath the surface rocks gave way to slippery darkness. She stepped back as if she might fall.

'Aphrodite was so completely spellbound by Adonis's beauty that she couldn't bear to be parted from him. She had to share him with Persephone, the goddess of death, for six months each year.'

'Children aren't parcels to be passed around,' said Coral indignantly.

'Indeed,' he said, his voice low and calm. 'But no one argued with Zeus.'

'I'd give it a try!' she smiled.

'Yes. I imagine you would,' he said quietly.

He'd removed his sunglasses and was standing close by, watching her. She smiled into the heavy silence and then found herself staring, mesmerised by the navy rings around ice-blue irises and the high cheekbones that seemed slightly flushed underneath the honey skin. The close-cropped beard that framed his mouth…

That mouth. She so badly wanted to photograph the absolute perfection of it—wanted to touch and mould it with her fingers.

Wow. He was the real deal and no mistake.

'You were saying something about being inspired by Greek mythology?'

She snapped out of her reverie. He was beginning to sound impatient, but before she could answer she heard music. The silly ringtone she'd set for her mother's calls. The only ones she answered, regardless of where she was or who she was with.

'Excuse me,' she said, reaching for her bag. 'My phone's ringing.'

'You can call them back. This won't take long.'

Her fingers closed around her phone. Maybe now wasn't the best time to argue. Surely her mum would know she was busy and would call back...

'Sure,' she said.

She smiled sweetly and turned to see him pointing at a perfect lounge with an ornate love seat. Her shoes squeaked on the marble floor as she walked and she was intensely aware of how casual she looked in her favourite fifties sundress. She'd hoped vintage would cut it among the fashionistas, but around all this money she simply felt shabby.

Not everyone is born with a silver spoon in their mouth, she thought defensively.

Gathering her skirt, she sat, intensely aware of him watching. His eyes flicked over her, but still his face remained impassive.

'I'll be honest. Your concept does not sound innovative or new.'

Oh, great...

He pinned her with his intense blue gaze. She forced herself to look right at him.

'The Greek goddess thing has been done to death. Kyla is an Australian marrying into Italian nobility. I thought with your youth you might bring a fresh approach.'

'I'm sure I can do fresh. I've got loads more ideas—'

'Your portfolio contained high fashion—art. Very beautiful. Intelligent. But this feature needs to be something much more glamorous. *Heavenly* readers deserve a twenty-first-century fairytale.'

'Absolutely. A prince marrying his Cinderella.'

He sighed impatiently.

She swallowed. *Come on, Coral!* This was going badly wrong. She'd put in so much work. There was no way she was going to let it fall apart now. She *had* to pull it back.

'If you could tell me more about what you have in mind I'm sure I can deliver.'

Her phone started to ring again. She glanced at her bag. Her mother would be getting in a panic. They hadn't seen or spoken to each other for two days now. And she was hundreds of miles away on an island, on the cusp of what might be the most important move in her career.

Or the worst.

'Sorry, I thought I'd put it on silent. Would you mind if I took the call?'

'Don't you think you're a little busy right now?'

She squirmed on the seat and tried to put it out of her mind.

'Signor Rossini, I will deliver exactly what you want. When I set my mind to something I don't give up until I succeed—'

He cut her off. 'The photographers I work with are legendary.'

He wasn't even giving her a chance. It was as if he had made his mind up already—and that was just plain unfair.

'Everyone's got to start somewhere! I only found out what the commission was two hours ago, if you'll recall?'

'Maybe so, but I would have thought that on the flight over you would have worked up your ideas.'

'This is not how I would expect to carry out a commission. There should be consultation and discussion, and various themes explored with the client. Not two hours' notice and then an interview that feels more like an interrogation.'

'This feels like an interrogation?'

She swallowed, regretting her brave words. But she couldn't take them back.

'If you feel that this is an interrogation, you'd better get a new career. This is business—*and* it's personal. As owner of *Heavenly*, I am simply making sure that a complete novice gives me the quality of work and the discretion I require. I have never met you. I have no guarantees about you. No recommendations other than Mariella's and the words that come out of your mouth. So far they're not up to my standards. You understand my concern?'

His tone was so quiet, so controlled.

The phone. *Again.*

'If you'd rather chat on the phone, be my guest.'

He was mocking her now. She dipped her hand into her bag, faced him grimly and grabbed her phone.

'I'm taking this,' she said, then turned her head slightly. 'Mum, I'm fine. Yes, everything is fine. I can't talk now because I'm being interviewed. Hydros—the island is Hydros. There's no need to panic. You'll only get yourself upset. I'll call you right back. I won't be long. I promise.'

He watched, one eyebrow raised, as she switched the phone off and then put it back in her bag. Her face was flushed, but the burn she felt on her cheeks was nothing to what she felt in her chest.

'I'm sorry,' she said, 'but it's my mother. I had to tell her where I was. She gets worried about me and she can be quite ill with nerves. I know this was all supposed to be kept hush-hush, with your non-disclosure forms, but I've never gone to the end of the road without letting her know before. Maybe that's not how your "legends" would behave, but that's how we are.'

He looked utterly impassive and she felt the tension inside her bubble higher.

'You know, you're not the only one who cares about their family,' she said, filling the hideously blooming silence as he continued to watch her. 'My family is every bit as important to me as yours is to you. So my clothes are from a charity shop and not couture? So what? That woman on the phone is my mother. And, since this interview doesn't seem to be going anywhere, I'll head back to England to see her right now.'

She stood up.

'Sit down,' he said.

Despite the glare she fixed him with her legs buckled and she sank back down, bracing herself for his verdict. Her eyes flicked away, over his shoulder, to the other end of the cove, where the majestic old Villa Di Visconti sat against a hillside of olive groves.

The team would be getting it ready for the shoot. She desperately wanted to stay with them and complete her first big job, but she wouldn't be bullied into ignoring her mother when she needed her. Not by anyone.

'First of all, *I* make the decisions about who comes and goes from this island. The only way on and off is by *my* boat or *my* plane. So forget any plans you have for dramatic exits. Unless you'd like to take your chances swimming to the mainland?'

Coral's mouth tightened. No way was he going to threaten her.

'Secondly, respect is non-negotiable if we are to have any kind of relationship. You will never speak to me like that again.'

'Relationship?' she spluttered.

'Relationship,' he repeated, his tone now rich and velvety. 'As in client and creative.'

'I don't get it…'

He sighed, almost imperceptibly, and sat down opposite her.

'Let's just say you've passed the first test.'

'I have?' Coral's bag slid from her lap and her shoulders slumped. She felt her mouth hang open. 'How come? What did I say? The seventies thing?'

Suddenly his face relaxed, and for a second a tiny smile curved the corner of his mouth.

'Definitely not the seventies thing. No. Your loyalty. Family values. Very strong. And for me that is a pretty good indication of a person. I know you can take pictures, so we can work with the rest.' He waved his hand dismissively.

'I don't understand,' she whispered, staring. 'You're hiring me but you don't like my ideas?'

'Let's just say that I'm confident you won't let me down. What you feel for your mother mirrors what I feel for *la famiglia* Di Visconti. As long as you are sensitive to that, I think we will be able to work together.'

'I don't know what to say. This is all very—'

'Say nothing. Just convince me now that you can work the magic you say you're capable of.'

'OK,' she said, sinking back into the seat a little. 'It shouldn't be difficult. All the ingredients are there already. They're a lovely couple.'

He regarded her silently. 'There are some quite important differences. The Di Viscontis do not court the media. But Kyla is…shrewd. She wants to create an empire—for the world to witness every moment of her life. It is my job to control what the world sees.'

He sat forward, leaned his elbows on his hands and stared with such intensity that she had to fight the urge to slide back in the seat.

'Giancarlo spent the last twenty years of his life making sure that his family were undisturbed by the world. He adopted me when I was eight, so I think I'm in a good place to judge. There's no way I'm going to let the family's privacy unravel because of someone's vanity.'

Coral sat up and blinked. His emotion was completely under control, but she could feel the passion and the warning in the words that he spoke.

She nodded. 'I didn't realise. I thought you were his son...' Her voice trailed off. 'Not that it's any of my business.'

'Correct. It's not your business, but it *is* public knowledge. I was at school with Salvatore, in Switzerland. We were waiting for our parents to collect us for the Christmas vacation but mine never came. I was eight. They were late because my mother had to fulfil other commitments—an interview. She was an actress and had a new film to promote. And then bad weather came down. She and my father were killed in an avalanche on the way.'

'Oh, my God, I'm so sorry. Really.'

'Don't apologise. I was scooped up by Giancarlo the day it happened and he looked after me ever since. I've been blessed beyond words to be part of this family, so you understand now why I don't want the Di Visconti name to be tainted by this—'

'Fairytale?'

'Charade,' he said, watching her closely. 'I want it stage-managed down to the last dusting of powder on Kyla's cheeks.'

'So you're not really bothered about the art? This is all about making sure no one will kiss and tell or show your family in a bad light.'

'I *know* that no one will kiss and tell because I would slap an injunction on them and on any publication stupid enough to print it. Have no doubt about that, *signorina*.'

'I hope you're not implying that I would do something like that? I'm here because I want a proper career as a photographer. I'm not in it for the fame.'

He stared at her, and for the first time some emotion

flickered in his eyes. It was so intense she couldn't hold his gaze. She looked down at her lap, at her crushed and crumpled dress, the scuffed peep-toe sandals, her shabby bag.

'I'm only saying that I've got my principles too,' she said quietly.

After a long moment he stood up, his hands on his hips. He watched her, then nodded. 'I think we understand each other. I suggest we get some lunch and then I'll show you around. You can tell me a bit more about yourself and your ideas about fairytales. Let's call it part two of the "interrogation".'

She let out the long, slow breath she'd been holding in. Maybe things would turn out heavenly for her after all.

'Sounds good,' she said, swallowing the smile that was spreading from her chest. 'Though maybe we could leave out the interrogation part? I respond better to the carrot than the stick.'

'We'll see,' he said, and it was as if some kind of mask had suddenly slipped from his face.

He walked to the doors that opened onto the terrace and turned, fixing her with the most devastating smile.

'If that's what gets results, why not?'

She beamed back at him—a completely involuntary reaction, but the only one imaginable in the full glow of that smile.

He was so handsome it almost hurt to look at him. She could totally see why the team were falling over themselves to impress him. A date with 'Raffa' would be like dining on ambrosia. Everything else would taste like dust afterwards. Thank goodness theirs was definitely going to be a strictly professional relationship.

They walked across the terrace and took a short flight of steps side by side down to a beautiful dining area. Under an arbour planted with climbers, popping with bursts of pink and white, stood a long table draped in white linen, heaving under the weight of baskets and bowls of the most delicious-looking food.

'This is amazing. What an incredible view.'

'You know you're not totally in the clear yet? I'm still waiting to hear something better than your seventies goddess idea.'

He pulled out a chair for her, waiting as she walked over.

'The Greek *Charlie's Angels* trope isn't working for you?'

She glanced up at him as she sat down. His eyes crinkled as he smiled at her little joke and it quickened her heart.

'You don't really want me to get the thumbscrews out, do you?'

'I don't think I'd suit them, thanks all the same,' she said, shifting slightly in her seat before she dared look up at him. 'I can think of *many* more attractive accessories.'

'Are you flirting with me, Miss Dahl?'

He was sitting down now, utterly relaxed, one arm on the back of his chair, head cocked, watching her. His eyes drew her gaze like twin blue magnets. His mouth was ever so slightly curved in a smile.

'What?' she said, flushing. 'I'm sorry if I came across like that. I can assure you that I don't even know *how* to flirt.'

She reached for her glass, which had just been filled by a server. Her fingers closed around the crystal, damp with condensation, and she stared at the pale golden liquid that sloshed inside, glad to have something to focus on other than the impenetrable, delectable Raffaele.

'I find that hard to believe.'

She flicked her eyes to his in a determined stare and breathed deeply. 'You can believe what you like. It's not my way, and I wouldn't have thought you'd be open to such an obvious approach.'

'I wouldn't have thought so either,' he said, lifting his glass and toasting her. 'But today seems to be full of surprises. I didn't intend that you would make it off the Tarmac, and here we are having lunch.'

'May I ask what changed your mind?'

He placed his glass down and looked at her. A long, slow stare that reached deeper than his eyes.

'Let's just say I liked what I saw.'

Coral swallowed. 'You felt I had potential?'

'I did. *Do* you?'

'Have potential? I'm biased but, yes. I think I can deliver whatever you have in mind.'

He flashed her another amazing smile. But just as quickly his face became impassive once more.

'Let's get back on track. We'll finish lunch, then go and find Kyla. She has her own ideas. I'll sanction the ones that are appropriate and you can take it from there.'

She dipped some bread in oil. 'Do you sanction *everything* around here?' she asked, as nonchalantly as she could under the circumstances.

'You really have to ask?'

She let the oil-drenched bread slide down her tongue and swallowed as calmly as her beating heart would allow. She knew he was watching her very carefully. There was more than the midday sunshine warming the atmosphere.

'Are you flirting with me, Signor Rossini?'

He put his head back and laughed.

'If it's that obvious I must be losing my touch.'

In all her experience with men she had never felt anything that came close to that moment. She'd known him less than two hours, but she knew she'd hit pay-dirt when she made Raffaele Rossini laugh unguardedly.

'Let's just say I'm no push-over. It'll take more than a free lunch in paradise and a commission from one of the world's bestselling glossies to make me fall at anyone's feet.'

Raffaele's look across the table was straight and true. 'If I didn't know better, I'd say that sounds like a challenge.'

'Not at all,' she said, leaning forward on the table. 'I'm here to follow my dream. And I won't let anything get in the way. You can count on that.'

His thousand-watt gaze still beamed down on her and she was beginning to wilt under it. But she wasn't going to show weakness. She brushed her fingertips together to get rid of some imaginary crumbs, smoothed her dress and sat back in her chair.

Then she slanted him a look that said—*Is that all you've got?*

He raised an eyebrow, put down his glass and stood. She raised her arm to shield her eyes.

'It sounds like we're on the same page,' he said, nodding. 'As long as you're every bit as good as you say you are.'

'Only one way to find out,' she said, rising. She nodded at the old villa. 'Shall we?'

CHAPTER TWO

IT WAS JUST POSSIBLE—*just* possible—that this ridiculous situation might not end in total disaster after all. He'd thought seriously about demoting Mariella after her catastrophic error of judgement. It was only because of what they'd achieved together over the years that he'd relented.

He knew the magazine's editor was still in love with him, and he'd been fond of her once, but linking this feature with their graduate competition proved she just didn't get it. It was not a 'cute idea' when it involved Kyla and her out-of-control ego. Not now that she was almost family. And not when family was the only thing that really mattered.

If only Salvatore hadn't gone into such a tailspin after Giancarlo's death. He hadn't coped well when his father was alive and he'd been in even worse shape these last few months. Now he was right in the middle of this new drama and it had to be managed.

Where Salvatore was concerned, damage limitation was a full-time occupation, but at least Giancarlo wasn't around to see it. He was barely cold in his grave, and he would not have approved of this fast-track wedding at all.

Kyla wasn't right for the family. She stood for everything Giancarlo hated—with her second-by-second social media presence, telling the whole world what she'd had for breakfast, turning pouting and preening into a full-blown career.

It was a useful lesson, though, and it had made him even more determined to keep his own women at a distance. Life was messy enough without consciously opting for an emotional double suicide. Especially with someone who was so clearly digging for gold.

Anyhow, he had Romano Publishing to take care of. And the Di Visconti empire to babysit until Salvatore learned which way was up. So what time did he have for women, gold-diggers or not?

'Oh, this is too lovely! Would you mind?'

He turned to see the young woman who had charmed him into this volte-face. He rarely went back on a decision, but there was no time to get anyone else. Plus, she was principled. And smart. He had a good feeling about her. In more ways than one...

It *could* all work out, he mused. He'd had no intention of having any downtime this weekend, but he'd just hit a home run of increased turnover in the digital wing of Romano, and—even better—started some pretty interesting talks with MacIver Press. If he added *them* to his portfolio he would be one happy CEO.

'I can't let it pass—I have to...'

She had stopped suddenly on the narrow path that linked the old villa with his house. Her eyes, dark as charcoal, widened with joy as she grabbed her bag and started rummaging for her camera.

'Honestly, if I lived here I'd get *nothing* done. It's amazing!'

She stood back, checked what she'd photographed, then put the camera back to her eye and took another shot.

'I suppose you must take it for granted, but...'

She was totally in the zone, oblivious to the world. It

was always interesting to watch creatives at work, but she was so refreshingly, achingly lovely that he found himself slipping back into the trance she had begun to work him into over lunch. A trance that had him imagining kissing that wide, sensual mouth and unbuttoning the little pearl buttons that held her full, high breasts snug in that dress. Undressing her and holding her in his arms and—

She turned suddenly, beaming. 'Isn't it absolutely *lovely*?'

He smiled back. 'Absolutely.'

She turned around, giving him another perfect view. In that sundress she was so evocative of someone. A young Sophia Loren? Maybe… Feline, but incredibly fresh.

'You must thank God every day that you live here.'

'All day long,' he said.

'Mmm, yes. How amazing to call this home.'

'Third home,' he corrected. 'I live in London and Rome. But this is my favourite family retreat.'

'Of course,' she said, continuing to snap pictures with her camera. She turned to take one of him. 'It's like being on holiday in heaven.'

'*Avanti*,' he said. 'There will be plenty time to take pictures of heaven later.'

'Hang on. Is that Salvatore?' She had stopped again and was pointing out to the bay.

Their yacht, *Silver Spirit,* was berthed some way off, tagged by the trail of a speedboat. Salvatore's speedboat. He had stopped and was waving up at him.

'*Si.* The man himself. He'll be heading over to meet the team. Let's go, Coral.'

She had her hand to her eyes and with the other began to wave back at Salvatore.

'Coral,' he said again, more sharply.

'Sorry!' She laughed.

As he started down the path, he struggled again to place just who it was she reminded him of. She had such an Italian look—wide-eyed, wide-mouthed, with auburn hair and creamy skin. An exotic, sensual cocktail. He couldn't think of any famous starlet that she resembled, now or in the past, but there was something, someone that jarred in his mind.

'Just getting some background,' she said suddenly, jolting him out of his reverie. 'It's not every day you get to wander along the cliffs of Hydros.' She grabbed up her bag and ran to catch up. 'Does Salvatore have a third home here too?'

'Salvatore would count here as his *fifth* home, I think. At a push. Kyla has plans for it. I don't think they will be here much, though. They prefer Sydney, where she is from.'

'You don't like her, do you? This Kyla? I can tell. I'm getting a definite vibe that she's not your cup of tea.'

They'd reached the paved area that marked the boundary of the old villa. He stopped, and she almost ran into the back of him.

'Oh—sorry!'

She stumbled into his chest. He scooped his arm around her and held her against his side until she'd regained her balance. She tucked neatly under his arm, soft and warm and...

Not yet, Raffaele. Take it easy.

He let her go.

'OK. Before we take another step—the ground rules.'

'Right,' she said, smoothing the wide skirt of her dress and looking up at him, those big dark eyes so earnest, so honest. Unflinching. He was used to people looking away from him, nervously avoiding eye contact. So many men were intimidated and so many women coquettish. She was unashamedly neither.

'Professional questions only from now on. And keep your personal opinions to yourself.'

'*You* don't, do you?'

What *was* it with this girl? Why did she speak to him like this?

'Coral, what I think about Kyla or anyone else is not your business and should not even enter your head. You're here to do a job. *Capisce?*'

She nodded. *'Si—capisco.'*

'Parli italiano?'

'No, not really. I've picked up a few words from films.'

He looked at her again and frowned.

'We will meet Salvatore and Kyla. You will propose your ideas, chat them through with the team, and I will give you the final decision.'

'You *do* know that Mariella has already decided that the shoot with Kyla will be done on the loggia? That does limit our options.'

'She has? We've spent over an hour discussing this and you didn't think to say?'

'You were a little busy biting off my head,' she said, smiling.

This woman was beyond infuriating. No one *ever* spoke back to him and here she was, staring him down and firing back with the most exhilarating confidence. She was easily the most attractive woman he'd met in a very long time.

'Are you normally this difficult?' he asked, turning back to the path.

'I'm normally honest, if that's what you mean. It wasn't my idea to play it safe.'

They emerged from the cliff path onto the driveway. Before them stood the old villa in all its majesty, its secrets about to be shared with the public for the first time ever. A Di Visconti home for centuries, but now just the backdrop for Kyla's vanity.

He led on across the terrace, helping Coral to step carefully on the worn marble. He knew too well the feeling of the hard slap of bone on stone, the trickle of blood from split knees, the sound of Salvatore's voice, laughing. He knew the feeling of the housekeeper's arms around his young shoulders and the ache of wanting to be comforted. Wanting but never having. Because his own mother hadn't been able to.

Sometimes he felt as if his heart was as cold and hard as that marble.

He pushed the heavy door open, feeling the calming press of the brass handle on his palm. The relief of air-conditioning washed over his skin, cool and fresh. A buzz of voices caught his ear and he frowned, turning to catch the source.

Behind him the squeak of Coral's sandals told him she was right at his back.

'Sounds like it's all kicked off without us.'

He led on through the lounge areas that led from the pool into the main part of the villa.

Kyla had changed too much already. The oil paintings and eighteenth-century Italian furniture—heirlooms that as an eight-year-old boy he'd been taught to treat with respect—had all been replaced with squat sofas in white leather and black and white portraits of supermodels in various poses.

On through the house, he heard the buzz and thump growing louder as they passed stucco-panelled walls, repainted cream over the elegant duck-egg-blue that he and Salvatore had been warned never to touch with muddy fingers.

Salvatore.

Since Giancarlo's death their relationship had been more and more strained, and disputes about the will were adding to that. It had been such a blow for Salvatore to learn that Giancarlo had left Raffaele in charge of the cruise line. It had been the last thing he'd wanted too, and as the empire's main trustee he would do his best to pass it on to Salvatore when the time was right.

'Darlings! She's here! We have our photographer!'

They stepped out on to the loggia and there was the team, flanked by muslin-draped walls and a haze of chatter and noise. On one side rails of clothes and racks of shoes waited to be rifled through. On the other side lights, screens and men on ladders attaching flowers to the loggia's ancient columns.

And, in the middle of it all, Kyla.

'Raffa! You've kept this angel all to yourself!'

Raffaele felt his jaw clench as Kyla walked towards him, fluttering her fake lashes and pouting. She was hot for him and made no attempt to conceal it—even in front of her fiancé.

And he, Raffaele, was going to be part of this charade.

He should be at work, focussing on Argento instead of slumming it with the B-list. Raffaele felt his patience snap. He wanted the whole thing to end. *Now.*

'Keeping to what we agreed, Kyla. I see you've made some interior design choices already. I assume they're temporary?'

She looked hurt, but that was an irrelevance. She was wearing a four-carat diamond and in less than a week would be joint owner of this ancient home. That would salve any wound.

He felt the light touch of a hand on his arm and a whisper in his ear.

'I'd be happy to get involved from here. It's all looking

good so far, and I guarantee that everyone will be happy with the results.'

He looked down at Coral's face, the un-made-up, un-flinching eyes gazing up at him. Again he felt the tug of something he knew, something he trusted. He thought of her confidence during their little interview, her direct, no-nonsense attitude. He thought of the stills that had excited Mariella so much that she'd dreamed up this commission as a prize. She'd rarely seen talent like it—sympathy with the subject, intelligence with the design. Exactly what Kyla needed to bring her back down to earth.

Giancarlo would be turning in his grave.

'You're in charge. You have the veto—whatever you say goes.'

'You're clear that this must—?'

'Reflect well on the Di Visconti name? Absolutely. There is nothing I understand more than that. The lineage, the heritage, the legacy—I'm all over it.'

'"All over it" is not what I want to hear. That sounds messy.'

She swallowed and closed her eyes as if—damn her—she were dealing with a recalcitrant toddler.

'I know what you want to hear. I've figured it out. Your family brand is "class".' She walked around him where he stood in the centre of the melee, lowering her voice. 'Kyla's is "trash" and you want me to change that. You want the bored housewives and the media snoopers to open up their copies of *Heavenly* and see nothing but a perfect airbrushed and back-lit image of the ancient *famiglia* Di Visconti. An illusion.'

'*La famiglia* Di Visconti is not an illusion. It is solid and serious.'

'It's classy. I will deliver classy. That's what the readers want, too. They want a glimpse into this fairytale world.

They want to see beauty and elegance and style. They want to feel as if you've welcomed them into that world for the five minutes it takes them to read the feature.'

She was electrifying in her pitch. As he watched her he knew that he could stand her in front of any board of directors and they would hang on her every word. Whatever happened with these photographs, this young woman had a fire in her that would light up more than just this photo shoot. She had a fabulous career ahead of her. He recognised the signs.

'And I will deliver that. I *will*.'

He folded his arms over his chest, looked down at her upturned, earnest face. 'Yes, you will,' he said.

'Si, signor!'

And, dammit all, he found himself smiling. Just for a second. Caught up in her infectious words.

Then he watched as she headed straight for Kyla, greeting her like some long-lost sister. Beaming round at Mariella. Quirky. Confident.

That hair… Those curves…

Yes, maybe this would all turn out OK.

All around about him people got busier and busier. Raffaele wandered outside to take some calls and keep an eye on Salvatore. Every five minutes or so he'd glance over his shoulder to see what was happening inside.

He shouldn't have to do this. He should be able to let Salvatore run his own life. They were the same age, had more or less had the same upbringing, but they were miles apart in terms of values. In terms of direction.

If he could walk away from all this right now he would. But he'd made a promise. He didn't need a penny from Argento. He had more than enough from Romano. But Giancarlo hadn't been stupid. He'd known exactly how quickly it would all unravel as soon as Salvatore was let loose with all those millions. Tying him in through the will had been a cast-iron guarantee of keeping Argento afloat.

But how much more of this could he stomach? He couldn't watch over every move Kyla made. He'd have to let them sink or swim some time. Legally, he was tied to Giancarlo for three more years. But morally he had him for life.

He glanced back inside the loggia. It seemed that order was descending.

The adorable Coral was looking through the clothes rails with Kyla and Mariella. Then she was organising assistants to move screens and lights. Laughing with the hair guy, consulting with the fashion editor as clothes were ruthlessly discarded. She was 'all over it' and no mistake.

'Is everything all right?'

He was still standing at the side, checking his emails, when she walked towards him, a glass of water in her hand.

'Only you look at little preoccupied.'

'Just waiting to hear good news, Coral.'

'OK. I think I've got it down. It's not going to be a pastiche or a pantomime. It's a simple studio shoot—nothing too exciting. I'm afraid you were right about the princess trope. That's what Kyla wants to be. But I've talked her into nineties glamour rather than eighties pop. Those prints we passed in the hallway—the Testinos—gave me an idea. I said I'd do an *homage* to the supermodel. She loved it.'

She was chatting to him as if he was an old friend. The glints in her hair were warm and rich and he itched to feel the heavy tresses in his hand.

'The team are amazing. I can't believe how fluidly they work together. I'm learning so much. I can't tell you how grateful I am for this.'

She dipped her head and looked at him with those bewitching eyes. Those bewilderingly familiar, bewitching eyes.

'OK, so I'd better get back to work. Phew. It's hot.'

She reached her arms up and twisted her hair into a knot. Her breasts thrust forward and his groin was shot with pleasure at the sight.

'Come here,' he said, putting his hand around her arm and drawing her towards him.

He took her jaw in his hand, gently moving her face this way and that.

'What is it about you? I can't take my eyes off you. There's something so familiar… Have we met before?'

It was possible. Shorter hair? Different clothes? He looked at her again. There was something so engaging and compelling about her—and, still at the back of his mind, something so familiar.

She stepped back out of his reach and he dropped his hand.

'Sorry, but I don't think so.'

He had to laugh at that. 'You don't think you'd remember?'

'Maybe. Maybe not. I'm not sure.'

Her eyes dipped, and for the first time he thought he saw the coquette. She was either the most naturally sensual woman he'd ever met or she was playing little games. Either way, he was beginning to get more and more turned on by her.

'Look at me.'

She lifted her eyes slowly, flicked him a quick glance and then dropped her gaze to the side.

'What's wrong?'

'I'm sorry, but would you mind if I got back to the shoot? I've only got one shot at this and I don't want to blow it.'

He put his hand on her jaw again and her eyes widened.

'You really are genuine, aren't you? You'd rather hang out at the pantomime than flirt with me.'

'Signor Rossini, my future is in photography—not in flirting.'

At that he laughed. A proper laugh. The sound of it startled him.

'I like you flirting. You have a very promising career in flirting.'

She smiled too. And it was beautiful. So beautiful that he couldn't stop himself. He wanted this woman. *Now.*

'Come here. I want to show you something.'

At the far end of the loggia a short flight of steps led down to a sunken courtyard garden—private and tucked away. It was the perfect place for what he had in mind.

He clasped his fingers round hers and escorted her through the glare of lights and pounding music, driven by an ache that had to be assuaged. He led her down the marble steps, walking briskly, barely aware of the sun splattering flower shadows on each side of the path, until finally spinning her round in the archway that looked out onto the jewel-bright sea. He could hold back no longer.

He clasped her face in his hands and stared down into those eyes. 'You beautiful girl.'

But as he moved to kiss her she squealed and stepped out of his grasp.

'I—I have to get back. They'll be waiting for me.'

He smiled with casual confidence. 'You can take ten minutes to check out the view.'

'That's kind, but it will set tongues wagging. They'll all think I'm down here getting it on with you.'

'That doesn't sound like such a bad idea.'

But she stepped further away, looking horrified.

'OK, Miss Dahl. If you insist.'

'I'm sorry, but I really want to make a good impression

on everyone. This is so important for me. I need to net-
work with these people. Some of them could open doors
for me. The last thing I want is anyone thinking I've been
on some kind of casting couch.'

He looked at her. She was serious.

'Nobody would dare to question you. You've been in
discussion with *me*. And I answer to no one.'

She looked vexed.

'You don't understand. I want this more than I can tell
you. I've never been rich or successful. My mum has had
to beg and borrow and steal to put me through college and
I can't risk ruining this one chance.'

'You're not going to ruin anything. Mariella is one of
the toughest in the business and you won her over because
of your talent. You've won me over too. That's a fact. And
we have chemistry—really explosive chemistry. You can't
deny that. I'm not sure why you think it's such a problem.'

'I'm not denying that I'm flattered. Of course I am.
But…'

'But?'

She looked away, uncomfortable.

He'd had enough. He pulled out his phone.

'*Va bene*. I've got work to do. Enjoy the rest of your day.'

He walked away, smiling. Casting couch! As if he would
need anything so obvious. A glance, a whisper, a word left
unsaid—that was all it ever took.

But he had to admire her principles. How refreshing.
And even more attractive. At least he could be sure she
wasn't one of those who thought a kiss was a declaration
of love or a proposal of marriage. Or a sign to go out and
choose a wedding dress or wallpaper for the nursery.

Ha! He laughed at his own joke. Wallpaper for the nursery! Words he would never say. Not even with a gun to
his head.

CHAPTER THREE

'THE STILLS LOOK AMAZING. Kyla is really pleased. It was an absolute genius idea.' Mariella, who'd been a little bit glacial all afternoon, managed to squeeze out a compliment.

Coral closed her eyes in a silent prayer of thanks as they checked out the stream of images for Kyla's final outfit.

'The whole day has been a dream come true,' she said. 'Everyone's been lovelier than lovely. Just being here watching would have been amazing, but getting to work with the best in the business… I've learned loads already.'

'Yes, I bet you have. All we need now is Raffaele's final approval and then we can really relax.'

There was no mistaking the tone. Coral looked away. Glances had been exchanged all afternoon, but so far no one had mentioned the fact that she had been alone with Raffaele twice over the course of the day.

'*So* lucky that he gave you his approval.'

'Yes, I couldn't be happier.'

'Amazing that you managed to change his mind so easily.'

Here it came.

'Yes, it was. You're absolutely right. He liked my idea and I'm so grateful to you for giving me this chance.'

'You know we had a thing once, Raffa and I?'

'Oh. No. I didn't realise.'

Could this get any *more* awkward?

Mariella's wily, exquisitely arched brows rose. 'Angel, no one who dresses in Sophia Loren's hand-me-downs is fooling anyone. You think you can get your claws into Raffaele? Let me give you some free advice. You're just some light relief between emails. Don't think that your fumble on the terrace is going to get you on some fast track to fame. There's a whole stable of little fillies like you, waiting for him to click his fingers. So take it from me—success is about what you put in, not about how well you put out.'

'I don't know what you think you know, Mariella, but I can promise you this: I am here for one reason and one reason only. I want to make a name for myself.'

'You already have, angel. You already have.'

Mariella winked at her, then shook her head as she breezed past, leaving Coral adrift in the swarm of people packing things away.

But she was right. She was absolutely right. This was her career, not a fantasy island adventure. Raffaele Rossini was not going to chase after her when she was back in London. She'd been a distraction this afternoon and that was it. He was off the charts and off the agenda in every single way. Every. Single. Way.

Thank goodness she'd had the strength of will to resist him earlier. It had taken every ounce of her resolve not to kiss him back. When he'd touched her she'd wanted to melt into him. When he'd held her face she'd wanted to close her eyes and slide into heaven…

But that wasn't why she was here. She was shoving open the door of her career. And it would slam in her face if she messed up.

'Miss Dahl?'

She looked up from the images on the laptop into the face of a very attractive young man.

'Signor Rossini wishes you to attend a meeting at his villa.'

'Oh! I haven't quite finished, and my things—'

'The meeting is due to start now.'

Coral looked around. Mariella and the fashion staff had disappeared and the clothes were being packed away. Only a few junior staff still wandered about, tidying up the loggia.

'Is it really important?'

He gave her an *Are you serious?* look and shook his head.

'Follow me, please.'

It would be fine. It was probably a meeting to look through the images she'd shot and select the best, decide what needed to be filtered or airbrushed. Mariella would be there. And the other senior staff. Maybe they would be planning the next shoot. There was talk that Kyla was going to ask Salvatore to do a couple shoot.

She picked up her precious camera and tucked it in her bag. Then she followed the brisk pace set by the man back through the house and out to the front entrance, into a black buggy and along the short paved road to Raffaele's villa.

Her stomach fluttered and she felt the dirt and dust of the day on her as she tried to wipe her damp hands on her dress.

'Do you think I could clean up before I meet Signor Rossini?' she asked the young man, but he merely opened the door and closed it behind her as she once more stepped inside the spectacular house.

'You may bathe in Aphrodite's Pool, if you like.'

'Raffaele?'

She looked around for signs of the others, but the eerie green glow from the sunken pool and the shimmer of light from the chandelier landed on a room that was quite deserted.

'Indeed. Thank you for joining me,' he said, beckoning for her to follow as he led her through the lounge and out to the terrace.

It was already lit with candles and tiny lights, and there was a glimmering curtain between the wide, low walls and the high hedges beyond.

'I thought it was important to close our discussion more appropriately than the last time. Mariella has just left. She thought things went very well. You have potential.'

'Thank you,' said Coral, following behind him.

Her eyes shifted from the broad slope of his shoulders in a tight T-shirt to the tight fit of his trousers across his backside as he walked. He stopped and turned so suddenly that she realised she'd been caught staring.

She looked up at the unreadable, unbearably handsome face and blushed.

'Yes, everyone seemed pleased,' she babbled. 'Especially Kyla. She channelled her inner supermodel and looked quite the goddess—but in a very tasteful way. I'm so glad you're pleased.'

'Yes, I am. Very pleased.'

He took the bag that hung limply from her hand and put it down. The butterflies in her stomach soared. To please Mariella was one thing, but to please the CEO of Romano with the list of conditions he had set was another thing entirely. She felt almost dizzy with pride.

'I couldn't be more pleased,' he said.

And, although she knew he wasn't just talking about her work, she was flattered.

'That makes me feel very proud,' she said.

'So you should be.'

He stared into her eyes and she tried to look away, but

the inky irises drew her in deeper and deeper. He smiled, ever so slightly, and her eyes fell to his mouth, to the perfect shapes and shadows.

Oh, my God! He's going to kiss me!

Her treacherous body fluttered with longing. But he smiled gently and the moment passed as he turned back towards the lights of the house.

Air flew from her lungs like a burst balloon. She felt light-headed. Undone. And nothing had even happened.

'You can bask in your glory all evening at the party.'

'What party?' she said, swallowing.

'It's been a good day. Kyla's lust for cheap glamour has been held in check. Mariella has pulled off a great feature. Of course there will be a party. They're getting it ready now, at the old villa. Salvatore is coming here shortly—we have some things to discuss—and then we will come over to join you all.'

He was inside now, walking back to the lounge. The dogs pricked up their ears and tracked him with their eyes as he passed.

'That's amazing. I mean, I'm really, really pleased that you liked the work. Do you think…?' She paused.

'Do I think that there might be more commissions to follow?' he said.

He unscrewed a bottle of water and poured it out slowly, rhythmically.

'Perhaps… Kyla has some idea of a couple thing with Salvatore, so maybe they'll want you to do that before the wedding. Mariella will talk that through with you tonight.'

'That's incredible. I can't thank you enough.'

Her mind whirred. A party. The staff would all be there. Mariella and the others, drinking champagne and looking so well put together—the way they always looked. They worked in an industry where everything was about looking perfect, and they had access to every product, every accessory under the sun. Her vintage thrift shop dress had been just about good enough for daytime, but she'd look ridiculous wearing it again tonight.

'I wish I'd known. I thought I'd be flying home tonight. I never imagined I'd be invited to a party. I've not brought anything to wear.'

'That's never a problem on a fashion shoot. Everyone will be helping themselves.'

'But I can't wear those clothes! I'm a totally different shape.'

'There'll be something to suit you. You're not such a different shape than Kyla.'

'I'm nothing *like* Kyla. She's tiny. I'm…'

Coral ran a mental check over the clothes that had been brought, trying to imagine herself squeezing into something that might pass scrutiny.

'You're…what?'

He sipped water and looked at her.

'I'm not easy to dress.'

'I'm not sure I follow.'

'I mean I have my own style.'

It was the best thing she could say in the circumstances. What was the alternative—pointing out her huge backside and overflowing boobs? *No way!*

'You will not be difficult to dress at all. Stand there.'

He tilted his head and scanned her body, his eyes trailing slowly from her neck to her chest and down to her waist.

He walked around her. 'Of course what you are wearing could be covering up some grave imperfections. Or perfections.'

'I'm well aware of what suits me and what doesn't.'

She watched his inscrutable face. He could be looking

at a lump of rock for all he was giving away, but she was feeling electrified as his eyes slowly scanned her body.

'The question is—what are you hiding under that dress? The perfect hourglass?'

He stepped closer and walked around her again. Coral felt her heart begin to thunder. She felt an unbearable desire for him to touch her with his hands.

'You know, my longest love affair was with women's fashion,' he said, lifting her left arm up by the fingertips and scanning her from wrist to shoulder. 'I remember going along to my mother's couture fittings. Even as a very young child I was fascinated by the process—the illusions that could be created or destroyed. That's one of the reasons I started *Heavenly*. It's all behind me now, but I spent my first two years after college working on American *Vogue*, copywriting. And dating models.'

'I'm no model, I can assure you,' said Coral, suddenly cringing at the thought of her generous proportions.

He had stopped behind her. She could feel the heat from his body, his broad shoulders and firm biceps framing her. She could feel the roar of desire rampaging through her veins.

'But you are incredibly beautiful. And you have a body that is driving me almost mad with curiosity.'

His words landed close to her right ear and she shivered uncontrollably. He moved around her, now lifting her right fingertips and staring down the length of her arm.

'As an artist, you will know that fashion is a creative process. But you should never ignore the fact that what is pleasing to the eye mirrors desire. For example, I've never been clear why it is that just this curve—may I?'

She looked down to where his bronzed hand moulded the space between her waist and her ribs. Her breathing stopped…her body seemed to wilt. She leaned back a tiny fraction and her bottom grazed his loins. She felt his chest against her shoulder blades. A wall of heat flamed between them.

'Why do some designers ignore the lines and curves that you have to such perfection—that instantly fire a man's desires? I cannot understand why they do not design clothes that flatter and complement nature's basic lines. So many make awful clothes that suit…nobody.'

Briefly he lifted her skirt, looked at the fabric. 'This is nice.' He dropped it and stepped away. 'Perplexing, isn't it? I could dress you. Very easily. There are rooms full of vintage here—couture and off the peg.'

He paced around her one more time, then stood right in front of her.

'The little buttons—mother of pearl?'

She nodded, unable to speak.

His eyes slowly travelled down, over her cleavage, and it was as if he had touched her. Her nipples hardened…her flesh longed to be touched. A tiny sigh escaped her throat.

'Yes, you really have got your own style—I love this fifties look. So incredibly feminine and sexy. I'm thinking of the perfect dress for you right now. I could send one over tonight. Would you like that?'

He was so close she could see the shadow between his lips widen slightly.

'Yes…' she breathed.

He drew his fingers down her arm, lighting a trail of tiny fires all the way to her core.

'Oh, yes, I could definitely dress *and* undress you…'

He stepped forward, cradled her jaw with his hand.

'Let me kiss you.'

She tried not to look again at the masculine perfection of his face, each line and shadow. He was right. Their chemistry was incendiary. Their attraction almost unbearable.

If she could just have a little taste, a tiny morsel of what he was undoubtedly able to give her…

Her body screamed at her brain to give in. But her brain screamed back.

'Raffaele, please…'

'My pleasure,' he said, smiling.

'We can't. People will talk,' she said, dredging up every ounce of willpower and stepping back, even though she was panting with desire.

'People will always talk. You can't control it and you shouldn't care.'

'But I *have* to care if it gets in the way of my career.'

'I can guarantee that kissing me will *not* get in the way of your career.'

She shook her head, taking another step back. A smaller one this time. 'I really want to, but I just can't take the risk,' she said, thinking of all the things Mariella had said.

'Really?'

'Yes. Really.'

He folded his arms over his chest. He was still smiling.

'I—I mean it, Raffaele.'

'I'm sure you do. You look very determined.'

'It's just not right. You must see that.'

'What I see is a beautiful young woman denying something very natural, very powerful.'

'I—I…'

'Yes? *I—I admit you're right, Raffaele*?' He gently mocked her, then took two steps towards her, so slowly. Her entire body erupted as he closed the space. He lifted her hand, put her fingers to his lips. Pressed them gently.

'You're going to have a fabulous career, Coral. Kissing me or anyone else isn't going to make one blind bit of difference.'

She stared at his lips under her pale fingers. She stared

at the perfect angles of his face, shaded with stubble. Her eyes drank in the image. It was mesmeric.

'What you achieve is going to be all your own work. But there's no reason why you can't have some fun along the way.'

'I'm not looking for fun.'

He raised his eyebrows, but he was still smiling.

'Fun will find you, Coral. A woman who looks like you? As talented and driven as you are? Fun is going to be all round you and you'll not know which way to turn.'

'That's why I intend to avoid situations like this.'

Her words sounded silly, girlish in her own ears.

He still held her fingers. She knew she should pull them free but she didn't want to. The sensation as he gently massaged each finger, stroking and soothing, was utterly electrifying.

'Avoidance is a weak form of defence, Coral. You're going to need to be much smarter than that.'

'And you're the very one to teach me?' she said.

He nodded. 'You'll be much better armed when you can tell the good guys from the bad guys. When you can work out who's safe and who's dangerous.'

'Why do I feel like *this* is dangerous?'

'I've got nothing to gain by kissing you other than plea-sure. That should tell you all you need to know.'

She felt almost woozy as he continued to stroke, his fingers now around her wrist.

'Pleasure?' she repeated.

'That's right. I don't want to manipulate you. Or stitch you up with a bad contract. Or promise to make you CEO. I just want to give you pleasure. Nothing else.'

He closed his hand round her fingers and gently tugged her towards him.

'Why deny yourself what you know you want?'

'I don't even know what I want any more.'

'I know you want me to kiss you—don't you?'

He moved a fraction closer. She could see the eyelashes that framed each eye, the fine line of his eyelid, the proud jut of his nose. She could scent him. No matter what her brain was saying, her body was reacting to this man on a level she'd never experienced before. She was almost completely lost.

'You can't always have what you want, Raffa,' she breathed. 'Or didn't your mother ever teach you that?'

He had been about to kiss her, had his head tilted to the side. He stopped and turned away. For just a moment she sensed his immense sadness.

'I'm so sorry,' she said, suddenly recalling his story. 'I shouldn't have said that.'

He laughed, but it sounded empty. 'As a matter of fact she *did* say that to me.'

Coral winced and crushed her eyes closed. 'I'd no idea…'

'It doesn't matter. It's an everyday phrase. People use it all the time.'

His jaw clenched and he shook his head. She swallowed. She'd really hit a nerve.

'I'm sorry,' she said, and turned her fingers in his hand, squeezing it. Then she clasped her other hand around it and tugged it to her chest. 'She used it with you and I understand how that must feel.'

He glanced at her as if to say, *Really*?

'It's nothing. I've been thinking about her a lot recently. It passes.'

He smiled, but sadness clung like a cloak around him.

'Raffaele…' she said.

He looked round and she saw the unreadable eyes, the

unbearably beautiful masculine face. The soul-deep passions and sorrowful secrets he held inside.

The tide within her swelled and burst. 'Kiss me.'

For a moment he stood still, then he stepped forward, clasped her face in his hands, lowered his head. And kissed her. Slowly, gently. The most erotic kiss.

'*Yes...*' The word came out as a sigh as he pulled his head away.

Her eyes fluttered open. He was right. How could something this good be wrong? What harm could result from a kiss? It was only a kiss. And it felt so, so right.

'Such a pleasure,' he said, kissing her again.

His tongue slipped into her mouth. Firm, but soft. Hot and moist. Teasing. Every touch enflamed her. She burned for him and wanted even more, her own mouth wide and greedy. She could feel the brush of his stubble on her cheeks, his lips damp with her kiss. He was the most amazing man and he was kissing her with such mastery, undoing her...

Suddenly the dogs barked. The door opened.

Coral gasped and jumped back.

'Ah, Salvatore. You're here,' said Raffaele.

Salvatore stopped in his tracks and stared.

'This is Coral. She is the "adorable girl" who has been photographing your fiancée all day.'

Coral hugged her bag to her chest and tried to smile. Salvatore was nothing like Raffaele. Shorter, darker, he had a full beard and darting eyes that telegraphed suspicion.

'Hi,' she said, reaching out her shaking hand. 'It's lovely to meet you.'

Salvatore turned to Raffaele, ignoring her. 'I need to talk to you. In private.'

Raffaele frowned, but his lips had curled into a smile.

'I'm sorry, Coral. I'm sure you can get to know Salvatore later tonight. And perhaps we can finish our discussion? The car should be waiting. I'll send something over for the party,' he told her.

She started to walk away, but he tugged her back and planted a firm, demanding kiss on her lips. Then he smiled and closed the door.

CHAPTER FOUR

THE GUEST VILLAS sat on the other side of the cove, accessed by a narrow cliffside path to the front, and a single-track road which led to the rear of the old house. Coral closed the door of her villa and headed along the path. A chilly, damp wind wafted half-heartedly, but nothing could dampen the exhilaration and excitement she felt at heading to this party. And about the opportunities that lay ahead.

With every step the borrowed satin slingbacks pinched her toes, and she drew the wrap a little tighter across her bare shoulders, shutting out the cool night.

Raffaele really did know fashion. The dress he'd sent was perfect, with its deep crossover bodice, nipped-in waist and full, flared skirt. A fairy godmother couldn't have done any better.

She looked up at the inky sky, searching for some sign of cosmic interference or a trail of fairy dust that would justify everything that was happening to her right now. Maybe it was the Greek gods' handiwork as they grew bored with ambrosia and nectar and started fiddling about in the lives of humans. But there were only the fat bright stars of the southern European skyline, sparkling like the huge jewels on Kyla's engagement ring, and the distant thud of bass, pounding as loudly as her heartbeat.

Only ten hours since she'd landed and so much had happened. The commission. The amazing lucky break with the supermodel motif for Kyla. But most of all simply convincing Raffaele. She'd never met anyone like him. So enigmatic, so alluring. But underneath as deep and mysterious as Aphrodite's Pool.

There was no doubt the effect he had on people was incredible—and it couldn't just be his billions. Salvatore was just as wealthy, but he had none of Raffaele's magnetism. She'd watched Raffaele at the shoot earlier: women fawned over him, men stood a little taller. He was the man everyone wanted to impress, the subject on everyone's lips. But the man nobody knew. Not really.

She'd searched online for more of his life story. It was simply documented. He was the orphaned son of the glamorous Lila Rossini, an actress on the cusp of superstardom, her life cut short by a helicopter crash. He had been adopted by the benevolent Giancarlo Di Visconti.

It sounded like a tragedy with a happy ending, but no one could really imagine what it was like to be in someone else's shoes. She knew that better than anyone.

No one would look at her passionate, artistic mother and guess that mental illness had plagued her for years. Always she was waiting for the mysterious man she loved to return for her one day. He'd never come, but her episodes of depression continued.

Four months earlier Coral had thought things were improving. A gallery had sold nearly all of her mother's last collection, and she was feeling happy about Coral graduating top of her class. But then—another breakdown. Lynda wouldn't talk about it, but she knew it was something to do with Coral's father. She'd buried herself away and refused to talk about him.

Even now all Coral knew was that he'd been her mother's boss. And that sleeping with the boss was a very bad idea.

Sleeping with Raffa was a very bad idea.

But she didn't have to worry about that now. She had her first feature in the bag and the chance of more tonight if she managed to charm the surly Salvatore.

They hadn't clicked. She'd known it immediately. Funny that the only strange, unsettling feeling she'd had since landing on the island had been when she'd met him. He wasn't at all what she'd expected—mean and miserable, nothing at all like Raffaele. But she had good chemistry with Kyla. And explosive chemistry with Raffaele…

As she neared the house music filtered out through the gardens, heard over the roar of the ocean. Voices rose and fell, high and feverish with wine and the knowledge that they'd all put in a good day's work and deserved whatever the night would bring.

She was going to make twenty new contacts. That was her aim. And that meant working the room as if her life depended on it.

She put her game face on and stepped inside.

It was busy. Everyone was dressed up and well on their way to a good night. Some people were dancing, but most were chatting in twos and threes. She searched the room, looking for Raffaele. But only to show him how she looked in the dress. To thank him.

She took a glass of wine and wound her way through the crowd. A few of the guys looked at her in a hungry way, but no one chatted her up. A few girls checked out her outfit, their stares dropping from her face to her shoes and then all the way back up. They smiled, but not with their eyes.

On she went, through the room where the shoot had taken place—now transformed again, with white linen-covered tables heaving with glasses and bottles and buckets of ice. And there, beside Mariella on one of the stone seats at the far end of the loggia, was Raffaele. His head was bent in conversation, and he was listening intently to what she was saying.

'Ah, Coral. You made it,' he said as she walked over. 'And you look very well. The dress suits you. The fit is perfect.'

He nodded, as if satisfied with his work, while Mariella raised her eyebrows over her glass.

'I wanted to say thanks for helping me out. I really appreciate it. I don't want to disturb you. I thought I'd try to have a chat with Kyla and Salvatore now. I can't tell you how grateful I am for the chance of another shoot, Mariella,' she said, turning to the editor. 'It means the world to me.'

'Not at all. Raffaele was just saying that you've delivered exactly what he wanted. Well done.'

She smiled sweetly and dismissed her, turning back to whisper intensely to Raffa. Coral's heart sank. Mariella wasn't complimenting her work.

She'd done nothing wrong. It was so unfair. She looked around. People were staring at her and then looking away. And it wasn't because she had overdone the eyeliner or had lipstick on her teeth.

Suddenly she felt someone brush past her. She turned. It took her a few seconds to figure out who she was looking at, but then she realised.

'Salvatore! Hi.'

He stood rigidly to let her air-kiss each cheek. She smelled a rather sickly cologne and too much alcohol.

'Enjoying the party?'

'Why, yes,' she replied, glad of somebody to speak to finally, even if he *was* a bit frosty. 'The villa is just lovely. And the views are amazing.'

He nodded. Said nothing.

'I saw you on your boat earlier—'

Salvatore's narrow eyes narrowed further. 'You saw me on my boat?'

'Yes. You must love boats—all sorts, I suppose. Do you travel on the Argento cruise liners? Ha-ha—it must be like hopping on a number nineteen bus for you.'

He didn't laugh. He didn't even smile. Coral played with the stem of her glass. She felt distinctly uncomfortable. She tried again.

'So this is where you grew up? What a beautiful house. And the grounds! You must have had such a fun childhood.'

'What's with all the questions? Why do you need to know? Are you a reporter?'

'Pardon?'

'Salvatore, Kyla is a little tired. She's asking for you.' *Raffaele.*

Coral felt his hand on her back and her nervous system instantly reacted. The wide, warm splay of his fingers calmed and alarmed her in a single move.

'Your new friend seems very interested to learn about the family.'

'Thanks, Salvatore, I hear what you're saying,' he replied. 'Coral is getting to know the family as well as she can before the shoot tomorrow.'

'No way! Seriously?' Coral's heart burst all over again. 'The couple shots? You want me to do them?'

Raffaele nodded, but he was absolutely poker-faced. 'Yes. I've just agreed it with Mariella.'

'I don't know anything about this,' said Salvatore.

'Your fiancée does. She has all the details and is sharing them with everyone down at the pool as we speak. She was very impressed with Coral's professionalism. Mariella and I both feel it would work well. It's all in hand.'

Salvatore looked from Raffaele to Coral and she was suddenly struck by how handsome he was, despite the frown that permanently cast such an unpleasant look over his features.

'It seems it's all arranged, then. I'll see you tomorrow, Miss…?'

'Dahl,' Raffaele answered for her.

'Coral,' Coral added, smiling as sweetly as she could.

'Yes, I'm sure there are plenty of things you will want to chat over tomorrow. I'll look after things here, Salvatore, since you've got your hands full with Kyla.' He manoeuvred himself to stand beside Coral, leaving Salvatore no option but to nod curtly and head off into the party.

'He doesn't like me,' said Coral, watching him retreat. 'If he's got a problem with me it's going to show in the pictures.'

'Relax. Salvatore takes a long time to trust people. He'll be fine with you.'

'And that's coming from *you*? He must be bad! Look how long it took me to get past *your* barricades.'

'Let's just say I'm more susceptible to your charms.'

She stared straight ahead. 'That's the last thing I want you or anyone else round here to think.'

'As I said earlier, caring too much about what people think will only lead you into trouble. You can go after what you want in life and still have a lot of fun. They're not mutually exclusive.'

She looked around to see who was listening. Raffaele stood utterly still beside her, surveying the scene in that outwardly expressionless way of his.

The party was now in full swing, full of cool, beautiful people, relaxing and having a good time. People who were at the top of their game, who were respected the world over. And she was part of it. She was barely out of college and she was right here, in the heart of a world she desperately wanted to belong to.

'OK. I'll admit that the kiss we had earlier was amazing. But that's it. We're both clear about what I'm here to do and what I'm not going to do.'

'As long as we're both clear.'

Coral couldn't be clearer. 'Completely. But I can't thank you enough—honestly.'

'You're here on your own merits. Despite what anyone may try to tell you. I don't suffer fools and I don't tolerate anyone incompetent. If you were either of those you wouldn't have made it off the Tarmac, as we've already discussed.'

She swallowed and looked at him. She tried not to, she really did, but it was impossible. The gleam of his shirt drew her eyes to the wall of chest muscle underneath. It was cut close to his body and she had such an urge to slide her fingers in between the buttonholes to feel the silk of his skin and the springy dusting of hair on the rock-hard abs she just knew would be there.

Forcibly, she drew her eyes away.

'I know I can do this,' she said simply. 'I won't let anything spoil it.'

'What could spoil it? You deliver what the magazine wants, then stand back and bask in the glory. Nobody is interested in anything else, despite what you might think. And if you don't want any fun—don't have it.'

All around her the party was kicking up its heels. She could sense hedonism taking hold. These people worked hard and played harder. And this was shaping up to be a night to remember.

'Looks like it's going to get messy.'

'What?' The music had suddenly gone up at least ten decibels. She leaned forward to hear him.

'I said—'

He put his hand on her waist, lightly, and pulled her

closer. She leaned in to listen and her lips almost brushed his cheek. Half drunk with lust, she glanced up and noticed his gaze on her face. Her body kick-started again.

'I said, looks like it's going to get messy.'

He indicated the room, where the music was slowing and people were beginning to grind their hips and dance as if nobody was watching. She saw two of the young interns locking lips. Hands were skimming bodies. It was electrifying.

Despite the throb of the party, all the women still slid their eyes to him. And even if her head was still telling her to step away from danger, her body was welcoming him home.

But then he turned his head and stepped to the side. One of his men had approached and was whispering something. He frowned, then nodded. Then they separated and he returned to her side.

'I'm afraid I've got some things to finish off, so I'll leave you here. I'm not sure when I'll be back.' He slid his fingers gently down her cheek. 'Take care, *cara*. The champagne might tempt you to have some fun after all.'

Then he slipped off into the party. Her eyes strained to watch him go but he moved quickly from the dimly lit lounge, through the loggia and out into the velvety blackness of the night.

Coral felt the loss of his closeness like a chill and hugged an arm around herself. But it was better this way. At least the decision was out of her hands.

She took another sip of wine and made an effort to mingle. The rooms were emptying…after-parties were being arranged. Those were not where she wanted to be. Much better to be fresh and full of energy for tomorrow.

And to sleep in a cold, lonely bed tonight.

She finished her drink and put it down. She grabbed her

wrap, tugged it around her shoulders, stepped past the few remaining people and went out into the night.

Buggies were waiting to take the guests back to their villas, but she was too buzzed to fall straight to sleep. She started to walk along the path, but a minute alone in the moonlight and she was regretting her bold move. Her shoes pinched mercilessly and the wind whipped at her bare legs. And she could hear voices ahead—male voices.

As the path opened out onto the road she realised these weren't some revellers having fun. The voices were angry. It was an argument. As she neared she realised it was Raffaele and Salvatore. And someone else—a woman.

'Don't be a fool, Salvatore. You're getting married in a few days. Either you call it off or you learn to control yourself!'

Raffaele turned to the woman. 'You—get to your villa and stay there. And remember what you signed. Because if this gets out I'll know the source!'

Suddenly, Salvatore lurched forward and tried to take a swing at Raffaele.

Raffaele stepped aside and caught him by the wrist. 'For God's sake calm down,' he said, shoving him away, but Salvatore swung again.

Coral watched open-mouthed as Raffaele grabbed Salvatore by the shoulder and threw him against the buggy. Salvatore bounced and stumbled back towards him.

'You think you're so perfect, Raffa? You might have the world fooled, but you don't fool me. You're no saint when it comes to women. You're just better at covering your tracks than I am.'

'I know I'm not perfect, but *I'm* not about to get married. And I'm not making a fool of myself in front of a bunch of strangers.' Raffaele's voice was low, controlled.

'Oh, really? You think I don't know what you're up to?' said Salvatore.

'You don't know what you're talking about. Go back to the house. I'll sweep up here.'

'Admit it! That little tart you were with earlier! How convenient that she landed the job looking like that.'

Raffaele grabbed him by the collar. 'I think you're forgetting yourself now, Salvatore. Go back to Kyla.'

'What else has she got going for her? You *never* work with amateurs, so what's going on?'

'Enough of your paranoia. You're drunk.'

He threw him into the buggy and Coral sank back into the bushes. It was too personal, too painful to watch. She heard the screech of tyres on the gravel and a mouthful of abuse.

Then nothing but cold, moonlit silence.

She stood staring at her shoes and listening to her heartbeat ease. Then she stepped back out onto the road—and right into the path of Raffaele.

He looked grim. 'You heard that?'

She looked up into his face—at the stern set of his jaw and the dark frown on his brow.

She nodded. 'But you don't need to worry that I'll say anything.'

He looked around, ran his hand over his right fist, which she noticed was bleeding.

'I know that. I trust you. And I apologise for the remarks he made.'

'Don't. He was just saying what other people are probably thinking.'

'You're still banging that drum, Coral? You really think that I would give you an opportunity because of how you look?'

He was angry. Even though he was speaking quietly

she could tell he was holding it in. He'd spent the whole day trying to button down the whole Salvatore and Kyla thing, only to have it all thrown in his face, so she understood. But he had to respect her point of view.

'I don't know, Raffaele. Some people might claim you would.'

'Well, those people are fools. I kissed you because I was attracted to you. I would have taken it further, but I respect you. Even if I don't agree with you.'

'I know that now.'

'Do you? Really?'

'But it's what others think that's the problem…'

'No, Coral, the problem is *you*. Caring more about what gossips say than anything else.'

'Don't you think that's a little hypocritical? What are you doing other than stage-managing Salvatore's whole life? Papering over the cracks so the world can't see the truth?'

He flashed his icy gaze on her. She'd really hit a nerve.

'You're very perceptive for someone so naïve.'

'I say what I see.'

'Don't you think *that's* a little hypocritical? The truth is more than words. It's about actions, too. Or lack of, in your case. I think in the old days a girl like you was called a tease.'

'Rejection hurts, does it, Raffa?' she said, stifling the sting of his bitter words. She wasn't a tease. She wanted him so badly. There was nothing she wanted to do more than give in to his magnetism.

'I wouldn't know,' he said. 'It's never happened.'

His eyes glittered in the moonlight. They fell on her lips, her eyes. Angrily. Hungrily. She couldn't look away.

'Hmm, Coral? Are you so sure you say what you see?'

'I try,' she whispered. 'I really do try.'

In the distance, the sea crashed home on the rocks. She shivered and pulled the stole around her shoulders.

Raffaele seemed to soften. 'Come on. I'm going to take you back to your villa now,' he said quietly. Then he took her hand firmly and started along the path. 'Before I want to take you to mine.'

They reached the door of the villa and she fumbled for the key. He stood back while she opened it and stepped inside, and then in the darkness of the hallway her phone lit up and started singing its silly tune. She ran forward to answer it, but it stopped ringing.

'Damn,' she said. 'Missed it again.'

'Everything all right?' he asked, stepping inside.

'Yes, it's my mother. I still haven't spoken properly to her. Do you mind?' She called back, but it went straight to voicemail. 'I can't believe we keep missing each other.'

He walked past her into the villa's small kitchen.

'Call her again. I'll fix you a drink.'

She sighed and followed him into the kitchen, throwing her little handbag down on the table.

'There's no point. She'll turn the phone off now. Blocking the world out. It's what she does.'

'Is there something wrong? Something serious?' he asked, reaching for two brandy glasses.

'You could say that,' she said. 'It's depression. When it takes a hold it's impossible to get through to her. She's an artist, as I told you. She's always had highs and lows.'

Lows that got so incredibly low nobody could reach her.

'Can't she take medication?'

'She can and she does. But it's not that simple. She won't get help for the real reason—the underlying reason.'

'Which is…?'

Coral hesitated. She never, *ever* divulged the reason for her mother's depression. It hurt so much even to say the words aloud. But for some reason, as she stared at his profile, watched him pour brandy into glasses, his arm flexing with gentleness and strength, she heard the words slip from her mouth.

'My father.'

She'd said it. Her voice cracked, as if the words were rusty, but she'd done it. The swirling grey mist, the anonymous man who was never discussed—there he was. The secret was out.

'What about him?'

Raffa cocked an eyebrow as he twisted the lid back onto the bottle.

'Well, that's it. I don't really know. She never speaks about him. *We* never speak about him. She finds it too upsetting, though God knows I've tried. In every way I know how.'

'I take it they're separated?'

He came towards her with the two brandies and passed one to her. The liquid burned her tongue but it felt good, warming and strengthening her.

'They were never together, as far as I know. Not really. He was her boss and he dumped her when he found out she was pregnant. She's never recovered.'

'I see,' he said, watching her closely. 'I'm sorry—that must have been awful. For both of you.'

She could feel a thickening in the back of her throat that had nothing to do with the brandy. She swallowed, willing the emotion away. This really wasn't the time.

'He's the last thing on my mind. I don't know anything about him—and, anyway, what could I possibly find out that would make up for what he did? Mostly I don't dig any more because I don't want to cause her any more hurt.'

They sat in the kitchen, facing each other across the table. Her handbag lay discarded, the phone's unlit screen like a beacon, reminding her of her mother's neediness. Quickly she picked it up and turned it face-down. Then she loosened the stole, touched her hair and twisted her bracelet around. Anything other than think about home right now.

'What about *your* hurt? Doesn't she realise that you've got feelings too?'

The thickening in her throat got worse. She reached for the brandy.

'Oh, it's fine. I used to make up stories to cover up the fact that he wasn't there when I was growing up, and then I went through a phase of trying to find out who he was. I read every letter in the house and went through everything I could find. All I know is that he was her boss when she first came to London. That's it. Anyway,' she said brightly, determined to change the subject, 'it's nothing like what *you've* had to deal with. I suppose this must feel odd? Kyla taking over the old villa you grew up in?'

'The villa? No. What's past is past. The present is much more interesting.'

He lifted the bottle of brandy, poured them both another drink, and with each soft splash of liquid in their glasses it felt as if the air was being cleansed, the ghosts banished.

'You look beautiful tonight.'

She smiled, raising her glass to meet his, grateful for the change in mood.

'*Saluti...*' he said.

'How does anyone resist you?' she said.

'You're the only one who's ever tried.'

'I'm made of stern stuff, Signor Rossini.'

He raised an eyebrow. 'We'll see.'

The soft light from the lamps bathed the side of his face in gold as the slight smile slid from his lips. Her gaze landed there, in that shadowy space where her tongue could slide. If she wanted it to...

'So, your photo shoot tomorrow—any ideas?'

She swilled the brandy around her glass and took another sip.

'Maybe something fresh and natural. We didn't use any of the casual clothes. That would be a lovely counterpoint to the high glamour of today. We could do it on the beach.'

She flicked her eyes up to see what he thought, but as usual he was giving nothing away. Totally unreadable.

'Do you have an opinion?'

'I do. But it might not be what you want to hear.'

'I value what you think.'

'OK. I think that you and I need to talk about this thing between us. You need to acknowledge that it's real. And that it's going to happen sooner or later.'

The brandy caught at her throat and she spluttered.

'I thought you were talking about the job tomorrow?'

'You know exactly what I'm talking about. You're deluding yourself if you think that we're not going to take it further.'

'You sound very confident.'

'I *am* confident. About everything. Always.'

He spoke so simply, so matter-of-factly, and stared at her so intensely that she began to feel the air thicken, making it hard to breathe.

'We could enjoy ourselves right here, right now. Or we could wait until you come to your senses and come looking for me. But it won't be long, *cara*. I can sense you right now. You're burning up.'

He was right. Her body had fired up with every word. Desire was seeping through the room like the scent from an exotic candle, flooding the space and making her languid with longing.

'Am I? You really think you're so irresistible?'

'I think you want me more than you're admitting even

to yourself. I've made you realise what passion runs in your veins.'

He put his glass down. She trailed every movement. The way his eyelashes closed over his brilliant eyes as he glanced down, then up. The shapes and shades of his cheeks, hollowed in the half light. The inviting swell of his lips as he curved them into a mocking smile.

'Since the moment we met you've wanted me to make love to you. You stood in my house totally undone and I could have taken you to bed there and then. But I respect you.'

Fire ran through her veins, lighting up every sensual area. She crossed her legs, squeezed her thighs together as her sex swelled and pulsed.

'Respect me?' she said, her voice a whisper.

'Of course. You're an intelligent, beautiful, ambitious young woman. You're amazing. And I want to make love to you.'

His hand slid across the table and lifted hers. She looked down at the long, blunt fingers, the strong, broad palm. A lover's hands. He lifted her hand and kissed it.

'Raffaele…'

She wanted to tell him how right he was—that she'd never ever seen a man like him. A man who lit up a room, who drew everyone's attention. A man who commanded not just one empire but two. Who looked after himself and looked out for his adoptive brother, even when his brother kicked back so viciously. A man whose life was cursed and blessed in equal measure.

Yes, she longed for him. She longed to see every last inch of his perfection. To taste him and make love to him. To have him make love to her.

But everything her mother had drilled into her, everything Mariella had warned her about, was right here in front of her. If she followed her heart she would have a night of passion. A night she'd remember for the rest of her life.

And then what?

She withdrew her hand and crushed her eyes closed. 'It's not going to happen,' she said, as firmly as she could muster. 'No matter how much you think I want it, I don't.'

'You don't? Well, that's my mistake. I'm definitely losing my touch.'

'Maybe I'm not a good multi-tasker, but I can only focus on one thing at a time. And right now I want to get my head straight for the morning.'

No, I don't. No, I don't. I want this. I want you, the voice in her head screamed.

She sighed. She felt as if she was standing at the edge of a precipice. Everything she'd ever wanted was on this side. But now there was another choice. A different path. And it felt so compelling, so completely and utterly right, to jump. To lean across and kiss him.

If only he would take the decision out of her hands…

But he was looking at his phone again, shaking his head.

'Of course,' he said, standing up. 'It's a big day.'

'Yes, I'll have a shower and then go to bed.'

She stretched her arms over her head in a ludicrous fake yawn.

'Night, then,' she said, but he had already put his phone to his ear.

'Scusami?'

He walked into the lounge, murmuring in Italian.

She pushed herself up from the table and wandered through the hallway to the bathroom, kicking off her heels. She felt her bare feet sink into the rug as she went, cursing and questioning and doubting what she had just done.

What if she had missed the chance of a lifetime?

Behind her she heard a door close and she stopped dead, listening.

She heard the murmur of his voice. Deep and low. Sensually wrapping round vowels like a caress.

She unclipped the crystal earrings and bracelet. She squirted lotion on cotton wool and dragged the eyeliner from her eyes. Then she unzipped the dress, slipped it off her shoulders and let it slide in a sensuous swoosh over her thighs to the floor.

She was in her best underwear—silvery satin balcony cups that held her breasts high and high-waisted, sheer-panelled knickers. What a shame he wouldn't see them. She turned in front of the mirror and twisted to the side, looking to see the perfect curves he'd said she had. Suddenly she felt very, *very* feminine.

In the next room he was still talking. She brushed her hair and let it hang down heavily on her shoulders, then closed her eyes, remembering his appraisal of her body earlier. How the very heat of him had made her melt. How his hands had skimmed her waist and how he'd stopped just short of her breasts. How he'd rubbed at her nipples with his eyes. And how they'd responded.

She unclipped her bra and released her breasts. Her nipples were pink and proud. Dear God, she was ready for his touch. He was right. She had been ready since she'd seen him at the airstrip.

There was no sound coming from the lounge. She paused, listening, but made no attempt to put on her robe or cover her nakedness. As each moment ticked past her body screamed for his touch. She should go back out there and find him.

She slipped out of her panties and walked slowly across the room, her heart thundering in her chest.

Her arousal was so strong now that her swollen flesh

rubbed gloriously as she walked. He was *there*, in the house. She could feel him, could feel his strong, presence. His energy. His desire.

At the door, she paused. She stretched out her hand. Her fingers shook with anticipation. If only he would come for her—she wouldn't stop what would happen. She would follow her gut instead of her head.

But she couldn't. She just couldn't. She would never forgive herself if it all went wrong. She let her hand drop and then turned towards the en suite bathroom. She would have to satisfy herself alone.

In the shower, she lathered her hair and her body with cream and looked at the suds as they slid over her. She lathered her heavy breasts, her round tummy. She lifted the shower head and rinsed away the suds, letting the water soak down to the dart of dark hair between her legs.

She held it there and the water drummed against her swollen clitoris. It felt so good, easing the ache that had been building for hours. But it was not enough.

She replaced the shower head and then closed her eyes and thought of Raffa kissing her. She slid her fingers over her flesh and sighed with the sweet pain. It was heaven. She touched the slick folds and rubbed a little more. She was so wet, so swollen… She longed for him to fill his hands with her breasts. She imagined him undressing her, undressing him. She imagined tearing off that shirt and sliding her fingers all over his chest, burying her face against his muscles, flicking her tongue over his flat nipples, nuzzling the hair that ran across his chest.

She rubbed harder, crying out with little breaths. In her mind she was trailing her fingers down from his navel, unbuttoning his jeans and then taking him, hot and hard, in her hand. It was long and thick. Then she was putting it in her mouth.

She rubbed again and ground out another little moan of desire. She was nearly ready…

And then the shower door opened.

He was standing there, fully clothed. His eyes were fierce with hunger. 'I'm watching you. Touch yourself again.'

Soap slid down her face and she quickly swiped it away. She did nothing to shield her modesty.

'I couldn't help it.'

'You were thinking of me. You want me to do that to you.'

'Yes…' she breathed.

'I can walk away, Coral. I can leave you to your own private fantasies or I can give you what you need. Show me what you want.'

The water powered down over her shoulders. She dropped her head back and let it course through her hair. She smoothed it away with her hands, over her breasts and hips. Then she lifted her breasts, cupped them in her hands, and offered them to him. It was the most provocative move she had ever made and she knew then that she was going to be changed for ever.

'Say it.'

She closed her eyes and let the words sing from her heart. 'I want you, Raffaele. Please. *Now.*'

In a heartbeat he was in the shower, tugging her soaking wet body towards him. His hands slid all over her. He cupped her buttocks and ground the hard ridge of his erection against her wet, naked flesh.

He grabbed her face and kissed her over and over, and then his hands moved up her back and round her ribs, until finally he cupped and kneaded her heavy breasts, rolling her nipples between his fingers and thumbs, moaning words in Italian.

Her head fell back as he crushed her against his body. His knee, soaked in his black jeans, wedged her legs open. He hooked one leg over his hip, totally exposing her.

'You must learn acceptance, Coral.'

'Yes…yes…' she begged.

'Don't fight what's going to happen.'

He thrust his tongue into her mouth, grinding her down with erotic assaults that she was desperate to absorb. She felt the sharpness of stubble, the dull edge of bone, the stab of lips and tongue and fingers, the moans of words in Italian, the red-hot wings of desire as she returned everything she could.

And then his hand slid down between her legs as he took one of her nipples in his mouth. Fingers thrust inside her and she moaned aloud as the golden ache of pleasure began to bloom.

'Raffaele—oh, my God, *please.*'

He hauled his shirt over his head and thrust his jeans off. She felt almost dazed as she stared at the wide, muscled shoulders and dark dusting of hair. Her hands touched his chest greedily and then she felt his hot, hard shaft nudge against her belly. All she could do was grab him quickly with both hands.

'Please!'

It was as if her life depended on it. She knew she had to have him inside her.

He knew it too, because he grabbed her up and slid her down, down all those inches of his manhood. She took them all—to the hilt.

Then she held his head to her breasts as he tugged her nipples with his mouth and rode her up and down on his shaft.

She had never in her life known pleasure like this, and the bloom of her orgasm began, rocking her whole mind and body with its intensity. She screamed and screamed, hearing the sound ricocheting off the tiled walls.

'I'm going to come. Is it safe?' he ground out.

'Yes—yes!' cried Coral, hearing nothing other than her pleasure as the final waves rolled through her and she collapsed forward as he, too, shouted his release.

For a moment they stood locked together, only their panting breath and the shower's steady stream of water interrupting their thoughts. Steam enveloped them. Their desperate need to have each other was easing, but still she clung to him, still he held her strong and steady in his arms.

'Are you all right?' he finally whispered.

'Yes…' she breathed into his neck, then his chest, as he slowly lowered her down. 'I couldn't stop myself.'

He lifted her face and kissed her gently, smoothing her hair from her brow and smiling.

'I'm glad you didn't. It was beautiful to watch, but I couldn't let you do it alone. Not when I knew it was going to be this good. It *was* good, *cara*. Wasn't it?'

She nodded and clung to his beautiful hard body. 'Amazing.'

He lifted a sponge and washed her down gently, cleaning and rinsing them both. Then he scooped her up in a huge bath sheet and carried her through the room, past her discarded dress and shoes. He cradled her against his chest and then lay by her side as he eased her onto the bed.

'I'll dry you,' he said, lifting the towel and softly pressing all the water droplets away.

She lay back on the bed. 'That was the most wonderful experience—I've never, ever felt anything like that before.'

He smiled and kissed her gently.

'Let's have some more, then. Come with me to my villa. I've got to sort something out with Salvatore—he wants to see me—but it won't take long. Then we can carry on. We have so much more to learn about each other.'

In a woozy dream-like state she slipped back into her dress and shoes and walked by his side out through the villa and into a waiting car. He held her firmly by his side all the way down the narrow road, into his villa and into his bedroom.

'Wait here. I'll see Salvatore and then I'll be back.'

'I hope he wants to apologise to you,' she said, irritated that yet again the surly Salvatore was making his presence felt in a negative way.

Raffa kissed away her scowl and watched as she removed her dress and shoes, rolled over in his bed and closed her eyes, falling into the warm embrace of sleep.

He'd lost control. For the first time ever. He'd walked away to take that call and then gone to get her, knowing they were going to make love.

Salvatore had left him a garbled message, weeping apologies and wailing about some new drama that he had to see him about urgently. As usual, he expected Raffa to sort out all his problems—immediately.

But he hadn't wanted to. He hadn't been able to wait for her any longer. She was unlike any other woman he had ever met. And it had felt good. It had felt amazing.

He moved the sheet over her.

Coral Dahl, he thought. The most passionate English rose he'd ever known. Driven, determined and with integrity a mile wide.

He watched her lying asleep. The auburn hair looked almost black now in the shadows of the night. Whoever her father was, her gene pool was extraordinary.

Suddenly he heard noises. He walked through to the front of house and there was Salvatore—like a swarm of bees, as usual. Raffaele wasn't in the mood for his restless, nervous energy. Not now.

'Whatever it is, it can wait. We've sorted out the girl from the party and I know you didn't mean what you said earlier. It's all forgotten. Just go to bed,' he said.

'Its her—the photographer. I can't *believe* you were so stupid. *I* would have seen through it straight away.'

Salvatore strode right into the house, his eyes almost yellow with too much alcohol and his face a contorted mask of rage.

'What are you talking about? Coral? See through what?'

'Dahl. *Dahl*,' said Salvatore. 'Don't you remember? That woman? The one who came after Dad with that fake paternity suit?'

'What are you talking about?' he repeated, more angrily.

Dahl... The name *was* familiar. There had been a Dahl once. An artist. A meeting. An accusation. Giancarlo flustered and furious.

'What are you saying?'

'Lynda Dahl. That bitch who claimed Papa got her pregnant. Tried to get money out of him. I dealt with her—as if I was going to let her get past *me*! Your photographer is her *daughter*. I've checked it out. No doubt she's come to claim her so-called inheritance while the will is still not finalised. I'm telling you, Raffaele, she's a con artist who's out to get us. She thinks we're going to roll over and give her some kind of pay-out.'

Raffaele's head felt as if it had been hit by a truck. This made no sense. The Coral Dahl who was lying in his bed was sweet and innocent and genuine.

He walked to the laptop. Turned it on. Typed in a name.

'It's Lynda with a "y",' said Salvatore, standing over his shoulder, watching.

And there she was. Lynda Dahl—artist. A doe-eyed blonde. A mouth like a bowl of cherries and milk-white skin. Forty-five years old. Exhibited a few times in London.

The mother of the woman lying sleeping in his bed.

'I want her off the island, Raffaele. I want her out of here. I feel violated knowing that she is breathing the same air as us.'

'Just slow down. *Stop.* Where are you getting your facts?'

'Facts? What more do you need? Don't you remember when I told you I'd found out?'

'Yes—you were twelve and snooping about in Giancarlo's study, looking for God knows what, and you found a letter. Yes, I remember. And I remember what I told you to do.'

'She came back again—demanded money for her daughter to go to college! Don't you see what's happening here? That so-called photographer has manipulated her way here. She's in league with someone at your magazine—she *has* to be! No doubt she's out for her own revenge and they've cooked this up together. Her mother tried the obvious way, and now she's trying by the back door.'

'Listen to yourself, Salvatore. Do you realise how paranoid this sounds?'

Raffaele's head was pounding. He was *never* duped. He had everything under control. It defined him. It was incomprehensible that this could have happened.

'We need to get her off the island. If I'm wrong, all that will have happened is that a total stranger has been wronged. If I'm right, we've circumvented a disaster. Raffaele—I'm getting *married* in a week. Can you do this for Kyla? For the family? If I'm wrong—which I'm not—I'll apologise. I'll send flowers, yes? Or jewellery. Just get the bloodsucker off my island.'

Salvatore's voice was carrying through the house, bouncing off the marble and echoing on every wall and surface. Splitting Raffaele's head open with his venom. His uncontrollable jealous poison.

He'd always been suspicious, had never been able to trust anyone. The only reason Kyla was going to be his bride was that her father's fortune was almost as big as Giancarlo's.

But it did sound plausible. More than a coincidence.

'Leave this to me,' he said.

'There's no time for you to work out all your angles, Raffa. This is *urgent*. Get rid of her and then we can work it out. It's what we should have done at the time. You were always so sure of my father's piety. Well, I'm not and I never was.'

Raffaele looked at his adoptive brother and friend. He had to bury his personal feelings right now. Feelings which ranged from cold, hard fury to bitter rage. How dared Salvatore slur his father's character? How dared he make these demands? But he was the nominal head of the family, and he had always managed Salvatore's insane insecurities.

And this one was about to play out on the world's stage.

The wedding was imminent, and if he didn't get things under control the whole family could be dragged through the mud, on every gossip page and on every screen.

'I'll deal with it. She'll be off the island by dawn and then we'll discuss it.'

Salvatore nodded and left.

How could his world spin like this? How could the solid foundations of his life be blasted to dust in a single moment?

Dust that *he* must sweep up—as he always did.

On the table below the mezzanine a gilt tray sat, with champagne and two tall flutes. He picked up a glass and held it in his hand. The crystal felt fine and delicate. There was a spot on the wall he could fire it at. Watch it smash off the plaster and shatter into a thousand shards. Hear the crash and tinkle and feel...what?

He had learned long ago not to let emotion show. He would hold it in until it dissipated. Until he didn't feel anything.

So they'd had wonderful sex? It wasn't the most important thing in the world. The most important thing was family. Even when it wasn't your own blood. She had hers and he had his. And until a few hours ago everyone had been perfectly content with how things were. It was always about family. Duty and respect and doing the right thing.

And he was damn well going to *do* the right thing.

Even if it killed him.

CHAPTER FIVE

CORAL OPENED HER eyes and turned her head. A lamp burned on the bedside table. There was a glass of water and a photograph next to it. She stretched. Her head felt heavy and her body languorous, loved. Heavenly.

She sighed and rolled around under the heavy cotton sheet, looking for Raffaele. She was sure he hadn't slept beside her. It didn't feel so long since she'd lain down, yet the night was so dark and the house so quiet she must have been out for the count for ages.

She got up. There was nothing to wear but the red dress she'd gone to the party in. She stepped into it and zipped it up, then slipped on the toe-crushing shoes. She had to pinch herself to make sure she wasn't dreaming. He must be waiting patiently for her. She should hurry now and find him.

She walked on through the hallway and along to the lounge. Her hair had dried in thick waves; her face, scrubbed clean, was dewy with sleep.

There was a breeze as she walked along the hallway, heels clicking, retracing her steps to the main entrance where Aphrodite's Pool glowed with its green half-light.

And there in the doorway, bathed in a swathe of light, glass in hand, stood Raffaele.

He turned when he heard her and she almost ran into his arms.

But there was somebody there—outside. He closed the door, blocking them out. He looked down at his feet, then at her face.

'Hi! I'm sorry, I dozed off. Has Salvatore been? Everything is all right for tomorrow? Did you tell him my thoughts?'

'I'm sorry, Coral. I've had to move things around. Change some plans.'

'Oh,' she said, her smile slipping. Something was wrong. *Badly* wrong. 'What things? What plans?'

There was such a chill, such coldness. She clutched her arms around herself.

'Has something happened?' He looked so unhappy she suddenly felt pain. She reached for him. 'What's wrong? What is it? Can I help?'

'Tonight hasn't worked out the way I wanted. I'm sorry. Tomorrow…won't be happening.' He turned away, took a drink from the glass.

She stared at him. Her eyes absorbed the fabulous body that she'd made love to, but somehow now it seemed to belong to a stranger. His face was drawn, but the proud jut of his jaw told her he wasn't suffering. Not the way she was, hearing those words.

'*Why* won't it be happening? I went for a sleep. That's all. You told me it was fine. You led me through to your bed. You laid me there and said we would spend more time—'

'I had you in the shower. I don't need to have you in my bed.'

Her hand flew to his face and struck him. She had never, ever hit anyone or anything in her life before. He held his face to one side, not looking at her. Coral stood, shocked, as harsh heat flooded her hand. She looked at it. She looked at him.

'What kind of man are you? Who *does* that? Who does what you did and then speaks like that?'

'I'm not getting into anything with you. You can keep the dress and the jewellery. I have no need for them. Your other clothes are already packed. Your bag's in the car.'

She looked around, trying to find something to hold on to, somewhere to sit. Something to anchor her in this madly spinning world.

'I don't understand. What are you saying? That you want me to leave? We had sex and now you want me to leave? I've lost the commission and I've to go? Is that it?'

'You can take your time. The jet is ready—the pilot will wait another hour or so. I'm sorry,' he added, finishing whatever was in his glass and walking to the doorway.

Coral stood in the huge unlit hallway. Above her, the chandelier's crystal beads tittered in the chill breeze that wafted in. A shadow moved across the doorway. Raffaele stood aside as the driver from earlier entered.

'Change of plan, Iannis. I will drive,' Raffaele said suddenly to the young man.

He strode over to where Coral stood and reached for her hand, but she wrenched it out of his grip and turned to face him.

'Don't touch me!' she bit out. 'You *bastard*. You are a thousand times worse than what they say about you. I can't believe I was so naïve—but I won't fall for it again.'

She scrunched up her eyes, as if the very sight of him was painful. And in a way it was. The worst pain she had ever had to bear. Those lips, those eyes, every inch of his face. His smile. And inside the coldest, blackest heart.

She stalked off in the high-heeled shoes, past the pool, through the doors and down the steps to the car. The scarlet dress filled the window in her reflection, screaming out how stupid she was, how cheap.

She'd been used. All it had taken was a dress and a compliment and she'd forgotten every single thing she'd ever learned.

Well, no more.

She turned around to see him standing at the top of the steps. Then she yanked at the damned dress, gritting her teeth and letting go a scream of frustration at the zip that refused to budge. She'd rather wear second-hand clothes for the rest of her life than feel she owed him anything. She tugged and tugged until it came down past her hips. Then she stepped out of the shoes and threw them both with all her might on to the ground.

There, in her nakedness, she stood, prouder now that she was out of his house and out of his clothes. She shook back her hair as she turned and saw him outlined in the glare of the portico light.

'Keep your stinking stuff. I'd rather go naked than touch anything of yours.'

'*Cosa fai?* Cover yourself!' he hissed.

He started down the steps towards her, and she saw fury and something much hotter emblazoned on his face.

'Go to hell!' she cried, facing him, unashamed.

Then she reached into the car for her bag, pulled out her own dress and heaved it on, glaring at him the whole time, daring him to say a word. Not bothering with the buttons, she slid into the car and slammed the door. She turned her face away.

Yes, she was proud. She could look after herself. Every time. And he would never, ever see the tears that flowed unstoppably from her eyes, or the hole in her heart from trusting too much and giving too easily.

The driver slid into the seat and started the car. In silence they drove. In uncomprehending misery she travelled all the way across Europe and back to London. The executive jet was at her disposal, but the cream leather interior was completely empty of any chatter or cheer. Or any sign of a fairy godmother.

She walked right past the car that waited on the Tarmac at the private airstrip. Walked past and kept walking, her huge, heavy bag battering against her back with each step. Her feet ached and she was miles from home. But she would not relent. Not even when the car purred alongside her, the window rolled down, and some faceless employee of Romano Publishing tried to persuade her to get in.

By eight in the morning she was outside the door of her little flat in Islington. By eight-fifteen she was fast asleep in her bed and by one in the afternoon she finally felt able to get up and make a cup of tea. Her phone was glowing with messages and calls.

That was the worst thing of all.

Most of them seemed to be from her mother.

How was she going to explain to her that she had made the stupidest mistake in the book? That she had jumped straight into bed with her boss and then been marched off the premises.

She had been given the opportunity of a lifetime—the chance to work with the best in the business, to get her name known in the circles that she aspired to belong to… Yes, she'd been given all of that, but she had ground it into the dirt like the butt of a cigarette because…

Because she'd got greedy. Because she'd wanted it all. The whole nine yards. The job *and* the man. And now she had nothing. Worse, she was in a minus situation—her reputation was in tatters before it had even been formed.

She made her third cup of tea of the day and then poured it straight down the sink without even tasting it. At least she'd made an attempt to drink the other two, but nothing—not even tea, it turned out—could make her feel better.

At six p.m. she steeled herself to read her messages and catch up on her voicemails.

At six-thirty she texted her mother a summary of the whole sorry tale.

At seven p.m. she opened the door and braced herself for the biggest guilt trip of her life.

She stood back, held the door open, put her head down.

'Oh, my sweet child,' said Lynda Dahl. 'My sweet girl. I am *so* sorry.'

'Please, Mum, please don't be sorry for me. I messed up. I'm so dumb and I really just want to put it behind me.'

'I could have prevented this. It should never have happened this way. I nearly told you so many times but I couldn't do it. I couldn't bear the pain all over again.'

Her mother was rambling. On top of everything else, her mother was having another meltdown.

Coral staggered back indoors, her head in her hands. 'Mum, just come in. We'll talk this through. It'll be all right. Have you been taking your meds?'

They were in the tiny hallway, halfway to the lounge, when Lynda stopped.

'Oh, my God, you think I'm having a breakdown. Did he get to you? Did he poison you against me?'

'Mum, what are you talking about?'

Coral leaned back on the wall. She needed to sit down quietly. She simply didn't have the energy to deal with her mother right now.

'Salvatore Di Visconti. *That's* who I'm talking about.'

'What? Yes, I met him, but it was the other one—his adopted brother, Raffaele—that I was dealing with.'

She was exhausted. Every word took such an effort.

'Raffaele?'

'Yes. I was supposed to stay to photograph Salvatore and his fiancée. It's a long story, but that never happened.

I took some pictures of Kyla—she was sweet. But the men were horrible. Horrible, nasty people.'

'So you met him? What did Salvatore say?'

She looked at her mother. Looked at her under the harsh light of the little hallway—a far cry from the chandelier she'd stood under the night before. Lynda's normally flaw-less ivory skin was blotchy and drawn.

'I don't know. We didn't really get along. He took some sort of dislike to me. And the other one—Raffaele. Mum, I'm afraid we—'

'Of *course* he did. He'd have been terrified the minute he heard your name.'

'My name?'

Her mother turned away. 'I can't believe that this is how you're finding out. I've tried for years to protect you, and now this.'

'Find out what? You're not making any sense.'

'I'm sorry, Coral. There's no other way to say this. Giancarlo Di Visconti was your father. Salvatore is your half-brother.'

'*What?*'

But as her mother closed her eyes and nodded some-thing finally settled into place, like a rock rolling into a gaping hole—harsh and heavy and immovable.

'Giancarlo Di Visconti is my father? I have a father?'

She turned around, aware of her mother's sobs and her arms on her shoulders. Aware of her warmth but unable to feel anything.

Suddenly the pain of Raffaele's rejection was eclipsed by the knowledge that the shadowy man—the parent with no name, the father she'd never had—was Giancarlo Di Visconti.

'I need to lie down. I feel sick.'

She stumbled back to the bed she had just vacated. She

sank down into the soft, still warm embrace of cotton and down. She laid her head on the pillow and clenched her eyes closed.

She could hear her mother in the kitchen, the sound of the kettle being turned on. As if tea would fix *this*. She almost screamed it at her.

Why had she never told her? Why had Lynda buried his identity so deeply, made her feel ashamed even to ask about him? Why had she shut her down at every opportunity, getting so upset that Coral had given up asking.

Lynda came in with two mugs of tea, the steam rising like genies from unstoppered bottles.

'Why didn't you tell me?' Coral sobbed at her through foggy streams of tears.

'Coral, you must believe that I only wanted to do the right thing.'

Lynda put the tea down and sat on the edge of the bed.

'He was married when we met. I worked as cabin crew on his private jet. I had just arrived in London. I fell for him. Everything about him. He was handsome and clever and urbane. He was ambitious and charming. Everybody loved him. I wasn't any different from anybody else. I knew he had a wife and a young child, but he was always travelling on business, always alone. For some reason he started to chase me. I couldn't resist. Who could?'

'*You* could! *Anyone* could! You allowed yourself to be seduced by a married man, for God's sake!'

'Don't you think I know that? Don't you think I feel ashamed?'

'I don't want to know. You didn't want to tell me when I asked you, over and over again. It was the one subject you glossed over. Have you *any* idea how it felt for me to have no idea who he was? You wouldn't give me so much as a name or a hair colour. I wondered if I had his eyes or his nose, but you wouldn't even let me ask the question. And he's dead now. It's too late. Oh, my God. I can't take this all in.'

It couldn't be any worse. All those years pretending her father was some handsome prince who was going to gallop back into their lives…all those years burning a candle for him. The truth was he was no more than someone else's philandering husband and she was the unwanted love-child. Except there had been no love. It had just been a dirty affair.

'I didn't want to tell you because I was ashamed. I was ashamed of what I'd done and even more ashamed that he didn't want me. He chose his family over us. He said he didn't believe me. Have you any idea how that felt? To have my love trampled into the ground? To be denied like that? Not only me, but you too. He denied *you*. And then he offered me money to disappear.'

'Why didn't you take it? Then at least we wouldn't have been so poor!'

It was all she could say. She wanted to lash out and hurt. She wanted to scream and shout and stop feeling the pain that was eating her up inside. It was too much, too awful, to feel the hurt of being hated.

'I was proud! Don't you understand? It was all I had. I had nothing else. A tiny baby. No career. *Nothing*. He was everything I wanted. And I was sure he would come back for me.'

All those years of poverty. She hadn't even had her own bedroom until she was twelve. No friends round. Her mother always in tears, unable to hold down an ordinary job. Paintings that didn't sell. In and out of hospital.

'But when you wanted to go to college I knew I had to find him. And I did. At least I tried. But I couldn't get past

Salvatore. Giancarlo was ill and they wouldn't let me meet him. I didn't have the strength to fight, Coral.'

Coral looked at her. Her poor mother. Pregnant by a man who didn't want to know. Bringing up a child all alone with no one to turn to. And with the might and the wealth of the Di Viscontis so public, yet so inaccessible.

'I'm sorry. I need to get my head around this.'

She reached out and squeezed her mum in a quick hug. It was as much as she could do.

'I love you, Coral. Please never doubt that I did what I thought was best for you.'

'I know.'

She sighed, comforting her sobbing mother. Soothing her and staring blankly at her tote bag on the rug, sunken and dead as her dreams.

She thought of that horrible man, her half-brother, remembering his rudeness both times she'd met him. How he'd seemed so brutal. She thought of the home he had—the yacht, the island, the jet, the wealth.

She thought of Raffaele.

Raffaele who had rejected her just like the Di Viscontis. What cruel twist of fate had allowed this to happen? He had been welcomed into the family that had gone to such lengths to keep *her* out.

She wasn't a Di Visconti. That much she knew. Giancarlo wasn't really her father. A father was someone who parented their child, not just someone who impregnated its mother. A father was someone who was there for you. Protected you. Loved you.

Raffaele had been fathered by him—she hadn't.

Her mind ran back over his glacial denial and the pain tore at her all over again. Was this because he had somehow found out? That made it even worse.

What a fool.

How could something that had felt so right be so wrong? Had she imagined those moments when he'd seemed to let down his guard? When his eyes had crinkled and there'd been the flash of his teeth as he laughed? It had felt secret. Special. Privileged, almost.

Explosive chemistry.

Well, it had exploded right in her face.

She sobbed and slept, and sobbed and slept. Night turned into day. Still she couldn't shake off the sick sense of injustice. What had she done to deserve it? She hadn't asked for anything her whole life. She'd won that commission fair and square. If they'd somehow found out who she was, why hadn't they welcomed her? She wouldn't have hurt anyone—she'd only been trying to do her job!

But, worse, why was she tearing herself apart when for the first time in her life she could finally put a face to the word 'father'?

It was shock.

She was in shock. Nobody would believe luck could turn so bad.

At least it couldn't get any worse. At least she knew now who she was and the circumstances of her birth. She'd made a spectacular error of judgement, but she could recover. She could get her career back on track. There were other magazines, other publishers.

There was no reason for their paths ever to cross again.

If she saw something on the news about the Di Viscontis she only had to switch it off. She could do that. She'd lived her whole life oblivious to the Di Visconti family and she could settle into ignorance again.

She and Lynda would be fine. Coral knew better than to judge her mother because, after all, was *she* any different? She'd walked right into the same situation. She hadn't been thinking about anything other than her own pleasure when she'd let Raffaele into the shower.

The only thing she had to pray for was the chance to put it all behind her. All she had to do was wind the clock back one week. To before she'd known she had this commission. Before she'd known anything about Giancarlo Di Visconti. Before she'd played right into the hands of the worst man alive.

She'd learned the hard way that it was all about her career and nothing else. So many doors would open if she had the nerve to push them. And she would.

Over the next few days she busied herself. She edited her website, uploading new images, and sent a slew of emails to potential employers. She went out on the streets and took pictures of cool boys and girls and began a London street fashion blog. She set up meetings with anyone and everyone who would give her five minutes of their time.

But after two weeks all she felt was worse. Her energy still hadn't returned. Her mother had hidden herself in her studio and today, as she trudged through throngs of people, she felt utterly and completely and desperately awful.

What was worse was that she could hear a tiny little voice at the back of her mind—a voice that she couldn't ignore any more. It was a voice that said there was a very simple reason for those tiny spots of menstrual blood that had stopped at just that. For the painfully tender breasts and the increasingly frequent waves of nausea that rolled through her body.

There was a very simple reason and it was demanding her attention. *Now.*

She stopped at a chemist on the high street. The automatic doors swung open and she stood aside to let a woman exit with her pram. Coral looked at the tiny baby bundled inside it and the voice in her mind got louder.

She walked inside and immediately her eyes flipped to the shelf on the left, stocked high and wide with all sorts of sanitary products and pregnancy tests. She lifted one down and her heart began to pound in her chest. Right now this was *her* issue, *her* problem. Or not. But as soon as she did the test the problem would not be hers alone any more.

She paid for the test and stuffed it into her leather tote, clasped it close to her chest and legged it back to her flat. Her fingers fumbled over the cellophane. She crouched over the toilet. And then she held her breath.

CHAPTER SIX

THERE WERE TWO things in life that Raffaele detested more than anything else. Deceit was one of them. Indolence was the other.

He opened the email from Salvatore and looked at the latest photographs from his six-month honeymoon with Kyla in the South Pacific, and their ten-million-dollar housewarming party in Sydney. Pictures of them drinking and dancing and doing not a lot else.

He barely glanced at the images, and bit down on the bile that had been gathering in his gut ever since that night.

He was good at that. Forgetting the unpleasant. He had almost completely wiped from his mind the fact that their wedding had been six months ago. Six months since Coral Dahl, or Coral Di Visconti, or whoever she was had blazed into his life like a comet and just as quickly blazed out. Thanks to him.

Salvatore hadn't given a damn about finding out whether or not he had a half-sister—as long as she was kept far away from him and his millions. That was what Raffaele had begun to realise. Protecting Kyla had been the last thing on Salvatore's mind. And the thin veil of patience and brotherly love that Raffaele had spent a lifetime keeping intact was beginning to disintegrate in front of his eyes.

The security team had uncovered nothing that they didn't already know. Lynda Dahl, a young, beautiful, struggling artist from Sweden, had taken a job as cabin crew. She'd worked for Argento and had definitely come across Giancarlo. There were pictures of him surrounded by his pretty staff in various locations and she was among them.

She had delivered a baby girl seven months after she'd stopped working for him. But there was no documentary evidence to suggest that the child she'd carried was his. That child now lived in Islington, London, and worked as a waitress. Her promising career as a photographer was not nearly so promising any more.

He'd tried to banish the whole thing from his mind but things had slid too far. The blind loyalty he'd felt for his adoptive father had been washed away like the tide on drying shingle, leaving behind a mess worse than any detritus. Giancarlo *hadn't* been a doting husband and father. He'd been a lousy husband. And the jury was out on his qualities as a father...

If only he could wipe his hands of the whole affair, leave the Di Viscontis to work out Di Visconti business. But he was mired in it. He owed Giancarlo everything. A fact that bound him to Salvatore more than any bond of blood.

And, more than that, he owed it to himself to find out the truth about Coral Dahl. Because the indolence and deceit he so despised in others were choking him now.

He'd discounted Salvatore's insane idea that Mariella or anyone at the magazine had had anything to do with it. The fact that she had won the competition had been a complete coincidence. She was a great photographer. It was that simple.

He was more and more sure with every day that passed that she'd had no motive to be on the island other than to take a giant step in her career.

He'd run over it in his mind again and again. Every word she'd said about Giancarlo. Everything about her mother. She had been desperately trying to contact her all the time she'd been there. She'd stated her hatred for her father but she hadn't named him. Had said she didn't know who he was.

She would know by now. The non-disclosure wouldn't last between her and her mother after what had happened. But there had been no attempt to contact him—no attempt to make a move, if claiming her birthright really was her big idea. But with her mother's debts and the meagre wages of a waitress there was no way she was going to turn her back on it. It simply didn't add up.

If Raffaele went to her it would inflame Salvatore's anger. He would immediately suspect a plot. No good would come of it other than to salve his conscience.

Whoever she was, she'd been a match for him. She'd taken control of Kyla's ego and delivered the best photograph to grace the cover of *Heavenly* in the six years it had been in print.

Except it hadn't happened. He'd pulled it. Ruthlessly and mercilessly. Without any explanation to anyone, he'd vetoed it. He had been just too angry, and coverage of the wedding the following week was all he'd been willing to schedule.

There were other features, bigger stories, better news. He'd told Mariella in no uncertain terms to find them and to make sure that Coral Dahl was never hired to work on anything connected with Romano again. *Nothing.*

End of story. Job done. *Finito.*

But it was nowhere near finished.

Burying the feature had not buried the memory. Or the increasing feeling that he had made a very, very bad decision.

Too many times he had listened to Salvatore, but this was going to blow up one way or another. It was like the string at the end of a stick of dynamite, and he wanted to control it when the explosion happened.

He'd go to London himself. The least he could do was offer her some kind of work. No matter how Salvatore felt about it, he couldn't live with himself if he left things as they were. And in doing so he'd clear up the paternity issue.

Within an hour he had cleared his inbox of emails. Within two he was on his way to the airport. And within ten he was sliding into the back of the company limousine and purring along the motorway towards central London.

His first stop was MacIver Press. The buy-out was going as sweetly as he'd hoped and it just so happened that MacIver was about to start recruiting. An invitation to present her portfolio ought to tempt Coral out from hiding and get her to force her hand…

Coral found her most stretchy leggings and pulled them over her legs. She rummaged in her drawer for something that wasn't faded or shapeless or too hideously dull. A red tunic with wide sleeves was the best she could find. Block shapes simply weren't *her*, but what else would fit the wide, lumbering creature she had become. Her fifties' skirts and cigarette pants were all consigned to the back of the wardrobe. And high heels…? *Forget it.*

She dragged a brush through her hair and rubbed cream on her face. She stained her lips with lipstick and added some mascara. A pair of small hooped earrings and a chunky bracelet and she was done. This was as good as it got.

After months of rejection—months of *no, thanks* and *not now* and *not really our thing*—and with her heart sinking at the thought of waitressing being her lifetime career, her luck had finally turned. An interview with a brand-new magazine for a small publisher. More art house than high-glam. Six months earlier she might have turned her nose up at it, but now she was grateful for the crumbs from any publisher's plate.

She bent awkwardly to pull on her worn boots—yesterday's grudging purchase from the local charity shop now that the November rains had arrived. That left her exactly fifteen pounds until the end of the month. Four weeks after that until Christmas and then she'd definitely be sacked. Who needed an eight-months-pregnant waitress in January? Absolutely no one.

Of course she could lift the phone and ask to be put straight through to Signor Rossini. Or she could walk in to Romano Publishing at London Bridge and demand a meeting. Or she could call the tabloids. Or a lawyer.

Because, yes, he absolutely *should* be providing for her and the baby. He should put her up in a flat and pay for the best antenatal care, hire a housemaid, a nanny, and a driver for the Mercedes. She should have the baby's name down for the right prep school already.

She'd thought of all that. Over and over again. Thought of letting him know that he was going to be a father. And then putting out her hand to ask for a fat wad of cash.

But history had a habit of repeating itself. So she wouldn't. She couldn't risk the chance of being told to take a hike. She wouldn't give him the satisfaction a second time.

She put on her raincoat, knotted her scarf.

Finding out that she was a Di Visconti had shaken her to the very core of her being. She felt untethered—afloat like a cork in the ocean. Everything that had seemed solid was now strange. Instead of feeling complete, she felt raw.

She'd always wondered, imagined, dreamed about who her family were. Visualised some romantic reunion with long-lost half-brothers and half-sisters and the love of a homecoming. But that was never to be, and now that she knew who her father was she felt utterly isolated, completely unwanted. Lost. She felt lost.

And her own child was condemned to be part of this. That was the worst thing of all. *She* could take any pain, but she would not knowingly allow her baby to feel even a fraction of the hurt she felt. The crushing rejection that had eroded every ounce of her confidence. The one thing on this earth that was driving her now was the need to shield and protect.

So there was no way—no way on this earth—that she was going to go anywhere near Raffaele Rossini.

He would have no part in her life. Or the life of her child.

But he has a right to know.

That stupid voice.

Her *own* father had had a right to know! And he hadn't been interested. There was no way she would face rejection again!

There was only one person she could rely on—herself.

She closed the door to the flat and went out into the street, dredging up every last ounce of energy she could muster.

Forty minutes later she was on the street outside MacIver Press. It was choked with traffic and people. She paused on the pavement and stared at the smoked glass doors of the converted church that housed her last chance. Through the windows of a passing bus she stared at the blur of the city. Everyone seemed to have somewhere to go, something to do. This was the world she wanted to be part of. This was where her heart lay.

Hugging her bag, she made her way across the road. She stepped up to the entrance just as two smart young women walked out of the building, chatting together. Coral glanced at their soft leather boots and city clothes.

She pulled out her portfolio and looked up at the imposing stone portico. She had to nail this—she absolutely *had* to nail this. Her mother was counting on her. Her child was counting on her. There was nobody who had her back.

She pressed the buzzer and stepped inside.

CHAPTER SEVEN

RAFFAELE STOOD IN the boardroom of this tiny but very precious jewel in his publishing crown and waited. It was almost eleven o'clock. Almost time for this gnawing mystery to reach its conclusion. Either she was Giancarlo's daughter or she wasn't. Either she was going to sue for her share of the estate or she wasn't. But, no matter what, he was taking the fight to her. He was tired of waiting for her to make a move. Because if he was sure of anything in this world it was the fact that he hadn't heard the last of Coral Dahl.

He poured another coffee and walked over to the glass walls. He'd had a busy, productive morning with the senior staff, talking about his plans for the business, reassuring them that there would be very few changes to the old titles, that his buy-out was not a wipe-out. All he wanted was to preserve what had brought him to the company in the first place: the weekly comic he'd read as a boy—the one constant in his life, devoured in secret while his world fell apart around him.

He sipped the coffee and looked down on the floor below. Cold November light flooded in through the stained glass onto the staff, scattering coloured light like confetti on the desks below.

At the back of what had once been the altar, above two empty sofas, hung huge illustrations from that comic—the ten-year-old super-sleuth Stefano and Petra, his faithful German Shepherd—pictures that he could draw himself from memory. Just staring at the inked lines took him all the way back to those hours under his bed, with his books and his comics, hidden away from a world he didn't understand, craving comfort in all that pain.

If even one boy got the same comfort he'd got, it would be worth it. Not everything in life was about making money. Eight-year-old orphans didn't care about that. All they wanted was to feel again the love, the warm body, the safety that had been ripped from their life. And when that wasn't there they'd look for it in other things—in dogs, books and in weekly comics that would transport them to other worlds.

That was why it meant so much to him that MacIver Press should be kept alive. The staff here understood. Fiercely loyal to the old characters and their art, they were more than happy to keep it going. But their business couldn't survive on the comic alone. He'd told them the price was a new celebrity weekly. None of the current staff had any experience or interest in this market, but they understood that it would balance the books. No one would lose their jobs and the brand would be intact.

All he needed was some competent staff to launch the new publication.

And, right on time, here came the woman who thought she might be one of them.

He stared down as she followed the receptionist through what had been the nave of the church to the rear offices. His eyes were drawn to her striding walk, her beautiful rich auburn hair, lying thick and long down her back. He felt his heart beat faster.

He looked closer. Something jarred. She looked like

Coral, but this woman was bigger. Had none of her style. This woman was *pregnant*...

He stared as the picture editor came towards her, smiling. The woman turned and then he saw the side of her face. The smile. Then she twisted round and he saw the leather bag, held close to her large stomach. It was Coral, all right.

In a trance, he crossed the room, pulled open the heavy glass door and took the stairs, his mind slowly coming to terms with what he had just seen. He'd known she wouldn't be a nun after their night together. So she was pregnant with another man's child? It was of no interest to him.

He strode across the floor between the desks. People glanced round from their screens, paused on phone calls. Ahead were the steps, the twin sofas, the pictures and her rapidly retreating back as she went into a glass-walled meeting room. Two more steps and he laid his hand on the steel handle, turning it.

As she looked over her shoulder, the picture editor's eyes drew into a frown and then opened in surprise.

Coral turned her head. Under dark lashes, her eyes lifted to his.

In that moment recognition was replaced by shock, then anger. And then, if he wasn't mistaken, fight.

'I'll take this from here,' he said.

Her hand moved to the strap of her bag, tugging it to her side protectively. A tiny move. He looked at the bulge of her belly, the jut of her jaw as she raised it. The picture editor dropped her eyes and slipped past him. He heard the door close.

'Hello, Coral.'

'What's going on? Is this your idea of a joke?'

He shook his head as he took in all the signs of her pregnancy. Even in shabby clothes she looked radiant. Her skin glowed with health, softening her features, adding to her allure.

'No, there's no joke,' he said slowly. 'We're launching a new magazine and I liked the look of your résumé.'

Her eyes widened, and then filled with defeat. But only for a moment. 'It was *your* idea to set up this interview? *You* own MacIver?'

He nodded. Then she turned right round, shamelessly flaunting her pregnancy.

'Seems like we're both catching up with the news,' he said.

'I didn't come here to shoot the breeze with you, Raffaele, so let's get that straight. If this is another attempt to humiliate me, then you're even sicker than I thought.'

'OK, I deserve that.'

'You don't deserve to breathe the same air as me!'

'I apologise,' he began carefully. 'I should never have asked you to leave Hydros the way I did.'

'Apology rejected. Your word isn't worth a damn to me right now. In fact—let's not pretend—we're only having this conversation because of who my father is.'

'Who is he?' he asked softly.

'You knew him a hell of a lot better than I did.'

He straightened up. 'Did you know you were Giancarlo's daughter when you landed that commission?'

'What difference does that make?' she said.

'None. You're right.'

She glared at him, and in those few seconds he took in the sweep of her hair over her brow, the unflinching, unapologetic stare, and it all fell into place. She might not look much like Giancarlo, but his spirit burned in her.

His eyes fell to her stomach. He swallowed.

'Congratulations. How far along are you?'

Her eyes flicked down to the side. He saw a small

movement in her throat as words hesitated on her lips. He looked at the shapeless dress, the outline of her bump, her breasts—large and heavy. She was pretty big, now that he really looked at her.

He looked again. *Wait a minute.* Maybe she was as much as six months pregnant? No, that could not be possible! That was *not* possible! She'd said it was safe! She'd told him so. Hadn't she?

She couldn't possibly be.

'Is that…my baby that you're carrying?'

He heard the crack in his voice at the same time she did and it shocked him as much as it shocked her. Her eyes flew to his, but he bit the emotion down, furiously.

'Answer me,' he repeated.

There was no apology now.

She stared—defiant, mute. Finally… 'Yes.'

Yes? His heart thundered into his throat.

'You didn't take precautions?'

Her eyes widened, she bared her teeth.

She stepped towards him like a fury. 'You mean *you* didn't take precautions! *You! I'm* not the one with the reputation.'

'You told me it was safe,' he said, as quietly as he could, almost choking on the white-hot rage that was building inside him.

She put her hands on her hips and shook her head. 'Don't blame me! *You* got *me* pregnant. Not the other way round.'

'I didn't *know* I was getting you pregnant, for the love of God! I thought it was safe. You…'

But he couldn't quite remember anything other than the passion and the pleasure. Couldn't actually recall her saying anything. Or him. This was bad. Too, *too* bad.

'Well, you did! And nothing you can say makes the slightest difference now. You're blaming me—just as I expected. I'm getting out of here. This conversation is going nowhere.'

Raffaele turned his head. The door was closed but even from where he was standing he could see heads bobbing up like meerkats, staring to see what the new boss was doing with the visitor.

'You can bet this conversation is going somewhere. We'll finish it at my house. Give me your bag.'

'Are you *insane*?'

'Pass me your bag and then we're going to walk quietly and calmly out to the front, where my car is waiting. I'm not discussing my private business in here with the world watching.'

'I'm sorry, I don't think you understand. What I choose to do has *nothing* to do with you.'

His jaw was almost locked down. 'It has everything to do with me!' he hissed. '*This* has everything to do with me! When were you going to tell me? Ever? Never?'

'However,' she said, as if he hadn't even spoken, 'if you'd prefer me to shout across the room that the father of my child is preventing me from going about my business, I don't have a problem with that.'

Father of my child...

He took that like a punch in the guts. Actually flinched.

'Do not play games with me, Coral,' he said, forcing himself to breathe deeply, to calm down.

Her skin bloomed pink. Her eyes flashed fear and challenge. 'You think I'm playing games? I've had more than enough of you and the Di Viscontis' games for one lifetime. So if you think I'm going to dance to your tune, you can think again.'

She lifted her folder from the desk and threw her raincoat over her arm.

'I'll call you when I'm ready to talk.'

'I think you'll find that your plans might have changed. You're not leaving my sight until I get to the bottom of this.'

'I'm wondering why you think I'll listen to a word you've got to say.'

Her defiance was unbelievable. Every fibre of his being thrummed with adrenalin. Every muscle tensed as she stood facing him, fighting him.

'You'll listen because we've got a pretty big problem to solve—and I don't hide away from problems.'

'You see that is why—that is *exactly* why—I didn't come near you. Because this is not a "problem"—it's a child!'

She put her hands on either side of her stomach, and as the fabric pulled back he could see exactly how big she was. How big the baby was. How many months had it been growing in her stomach while he was obliviously getting on with his life?

'*My* child!' she went on. 'And I will not have you or anyone else talking about this as if it's a "problem" or not wanted. Because this baby *is* wanted. By me. And that's all that matters.'

'Keep your voice down!'

'Don't tell me what I can and can't do!'

Two spots of colour had sprung to her cheeks and her voice rose as she spoke. He'd need to keep her calm or she might do something stupid. He'd already seen her temper in full flow.

'You're flying off the handle,' he said, as calmly as he could. 'What I am trying to say is that I will stand by my responsibilities. I will do the right thing. You're not on your own.'

'Well, forgive me if I jumped to the wrong conclusion. I wonder what could have *possibly* made me think otherwise?'

'I'm jumping to some conclusions myself. You turn up here—at *my* magazine—looking for a job, out to here with *my* child—or so you say—having had with no intention of telling me! Just what goes on in your head?'

'If I'd known this place was anything to do with you I would never have set foot in it.'

'Well, thank God for that, then. Otherwise I might never have known!'

'I hardly think you can claim any moral high ground. Your family is rotten to the core.'

'Correction. It's *your* family. Which I'm sure the DNA test will confirm. I'm only a member of that family through bereavement and a legal process, remember?'

'What DNA test? I don't need to prove anything to anyone.'

'Yes, you do. And you will. Believe me. And then I'll take whatever action is necessary. You've already proved you're untrustworthy, so you'd better get ready for court. I'm no Giancarlo Di Visconti, *cara*. I'm a Rossini, and if that's my child it's going to be one too. *Capisce?*'

He knew he was overplaying his hand, but how dared she? How dared she think that she was the only one who mattered here? From this moment onwards they would be playing by *his* rules.

'What are you trying to say?' she said, the slow dawn of horror now rising over her face.

'I'm saying that you will not leave my sight until I know if that child is mine. And if it is it will be brought up properly—as a Rossini. Not in some bohemian bedsit in London while you wait on tables for a living.'

'You might need tests, but I don't. I'm perfectly aware of the fact that I've got the world's worst father. But it's something I want to forget. Did I come running for his name or his money when I found out? *No!* And I don't want yours either!'

'If that baby is mine you don't have a choice!'

'My baby doesn't need a father,' she said. 'Certainly not one like you.'

She had no idea—truly, no idea what she was saying. Didn't she realise that a father's role was to protect and cherish and keep his wife and child safe? Had she any idea what world she was walking into as a Di Visconti, pregnant with a Rossini baby? In Italy there would be a media frenzy to end all others. And as for Salvatore…

There was absolutely no other option than to take control of the situation. If he was the father, his life changed from this moment on. For ever.

He paced towards her. She stood proud, her head back, flushed and feminine, fierce. But she was vulnerable. Completely vulnerable. He could see it in the tremble of her lip and the flicker of fear in her eyes.

He would make sure no harm came to her. And he would lay down his life for his child! But he had to be sure.

'Is. That. Baby. Mine?' he breathed.

And he waited for the longest second of his life.

She stared at him, and then it happened.

All the fire in her voice and her eyes flared and went out, doused by the tears that surged and flowed.

'Yes,' she sobbed. '*Yes.* And I did nothing wrong. *Nothing wrong.* But you threw me out of your house like a common whore. You're horrible! *Horrible!*'

The words were choked in her throat, but they were like spears in his heart. Her eyes were blazing. Her creamy skin was flushed and dewy. Her lips were plump and red. And her breasts and her tummy were round and full under her clothes.

She was pregnant. And he was shouting at her.

She squeezed her eyes shut. 'You're my baby's father.'

He moved to where she stood, hunched and sobbing. He put his arms around her and pulled her rigid body close. He didn't care if she pushed him away. He had to feel the life within her, had to hold her safe. To let her know that he would never treat her badly again.

'I'm so sorry, Coral. I know that what happened was awful, and if I could turn the clock back I would. I wish you could understand… We thought you were up to something. Salvatore was sure you were going to try to blackmail him and ruin his wedding. He distrusts everyone, and I accepted what he said. I didn't question it, and I've been furious with myself ever since.'

'But you were so *cruel*. You made me *hate* you,' she sobbed.

'I know,' he said, holding her, feeling the fight die within her.

He rocked her as her tears soaked his shirt. Her face was buried in his chest, her voice thick with grief. He held her steady as she told him over and over that she hated him.

And then he felt her lips on his skin, his neck, and his lips found her brow and her cheek. And then together they found each other's mouth and he devoured her sobs and her anguish. He kissed her gently and yet greedily, and felt the fire of his lust flash swiftly through his veins.

This woman was special. He'd known it then and he knew it even more surely now. He tugged her closer, absorbing the softness and the warmth of her body, full with their growing child.

She was kissing him back, and for a second he felt the world fall into place. Then she pushed. Her hands flew to his chest and she pushed with all her might.

'Get away from me!'

She shook her head as she gulped in air. She clamped her hand over her mouth as tears streamed down her cheeks.

'Coral, don't fight me. I'm going to help you. You'll have whatever you need. You'll want for nothing.'

'No, no, *no*! I don't want anything to do with your family. You threw me off your island and now suddenly you want to get involved? All those years my mother could hardly put food on the table. And now you want to know? I don't think so!'

She sobbed out the words and grabbed at her coat and bag. His stomach lurched. He understood how she must hate them all, but there was no way he could let her go.

'Coral, this stops *now*. I understand that you're upset about your father, but don't take me on too. I know I treated you badly. I made a mistake and I will right it—I promise you.'

He was ready for more drama, but surprisingly she didn't shout, didn't scream. When he finally moved a chair beneath her and urged her to sit down she didn't even pull away. He stood there, listening to her deep, soulful sobs. She couldn't hate him any more than he hated himself right now.

'I'll get you some tea. Would you like me to call anyone? Your mother, perhaps?'

She shook her head, said nothing. He spoke to the side of her head, which she now held in her hands, elbows on her knees. The folder of her work had spilled its contents onto the floor. He bent to pick it up.

'I know you don't trust me, Coral. And I think I understand why you didn't seek me out. But this is too big and too important. We can work out the past later, but right now we have to work out the next few hours. OK?'

She still said nothing.

'Look, you can ignore me, but you can't ignore this.

We have to make sure you're in good health. Are you still living in Islington?'

She glanced at him, drew her eyes away and shook her head slowly.

'I have an address for you there. If you hadn't come for the interview today I was going to look you up.'

She shot him a glance through bleary, tear-soaked eyes.

'Let's not pretend we're star-crossed lovers, Raffaele. I'm not so naïve any more.'

It wasn't much, but it was a start. At least she was communicating.

She turned now, took the folder from him and started to reassemble it. She still looked pale and drawn and desperately sad.

'The car is here,' he said, checking his phone. He reached out to help her to her feet but she shrugged him off.

'I'm coming with you because I have no real choice. *Capisce?*'

She grabbed her bag and her coat, walked to the door, down the steps and past the desks to the front door. Once on the street, she faltered. She looked around like a cornered deer, and for a moment he thought she was going to run. He caught her eye and in those seconds saw her fear and her hurt, and he felt the weight of what he was doing more keenly than if he had thrown her behind bars. It was going to take a long time for her to trust him, but it was absolutely the only thing he could do.

He watched as she sat down heavily and buckled the seatbelt over her belly. As he closed the door he saw her hand, bunched into a fist and clutching the cotton fabric of the tunic she wore. She looked straight ahead, saying nothing.

As they drove his mind swirled with a thousand thoughts. He had never come to any decision about parenthood. Had only thought that if the right woman came along he might marry her and then together they would plan to have a child. Not like this.

This wasn't just a pregnancy. It was the joining of two families—each of them with estates that would tie up their legal teams for years. Giancarlo's will wasn't even settled, and Salvatore's rage would be immense when he learned that he had a half-sister, and soon a half-niece or nephew. Legally they would all be entitled to something, and though Coral might be saying now that she wanted nothing, when she realised the world she was entering that might change.

His mind fired thought after thought as he battled to do what he always did and take hold of the universe, reorder it before it got even worse. But it felt as if he was wading through a river of mud, trying to get everybody safely to the shore, while they were all kicking and screaming and trying to swim in the other direction.

He reached across to close his fingers around Coral's tight little fist, and as his skin touched hers she glared at him and pulled her hand away.

OK. It would take time. He knew that. Just as he knew that he would do everything he could to win her round. There was no way he was going to let any harm come to Coral and his child. She might think that fathers were superfluous, and that was understandable after what she'd been through. But from his point of view the presence of a father was non-negotiable.

His child needed him. And he would damned well be there. Every day from here on in.

CHAPTER EIGHT

THE DOCTOR CLOSED his case. Two deadened clicks—one for each lock. He stood up, forced out some more breezy words, and then turned and walked away. Another click—the door this time. Footsteps retreated on rugs and wood until finally the house was in silence.

Coral lay back on the bed, closed her eyes and placed her hands on her tummy. She felt her baby—her boy—and recalled with a wave of sweet joy the little foot that she had seen on the screen, each little toe, the gentle bend of the ankle, his knee and hip and shoulder. His arm curled up and his tiny fist in a ball by his face, eyes closed in sleep.

What was he dreaming about? Was he having some innocent dream or had he heard all the things that had been said this morning? Had the baby felt all the strain, as she had done? Had he known his father was there? Heard the low steady burr of his raised voice, drilling out his icy instructions and orders?

And then he'd tried to make it all better by holding her close, making her feel just for a moment that he cared about her.

Of course he didn't. It wasn't love for her that had caused him to 'press pause on the rest of the week', as he had instructed his assistant. It was his duty because she was Giancarlo Di Visconti's daughter. Nothing else.

Giancarlo Di Visconti was dead and buried and past reproach. He would never be held to account. So his first lieutenant would sweep up the mess of the father just as he'd swept up the mess of the son.

The only thing she hadn't expected was that he really seemed to care about the baby. No, she hadn't expected that at all...

She opened her eyes and stared at the canopy above her head. It was a beautiful room, she had to admit, with the most lovely bed. Each brass post disappeared into a silk and muslin cloud. The mattress was high and she knew if she let herself curl up in it she'd feel like a fairytale princess.

To think that she'd lived across town in poverty while *this* was here. All the years of *not* having, of feeling trapped in their apartment, dreading the creeping chill of winter and the suffocating humidity of summer. Her mother's anguish over paintings that wouldn't sell, part-time jobs and summer jobs. Holidays that were a train ride, never a plane ride away.

Outside the traffic flowed in hushed lines past the park. She would be able to see it if she got up and walked across the Persian rug to the huge Georgian windows that looked over the private garden to the road and the park beyond. There were no noisy neighbours here, no litter on the pavements, no faulty lights in the shared hallway or damp on the walls.

Here, the scent of money hung in the air—more pungent than the fragrant bursts of lilies dotted in vases along the hallway.

She didn't bother to look round when Raffaele entered, but she felt his presence and became alert, alive. And hated herself for it.

'I had a word with the doctor. Everything seems to be well.'

The quiet, low voice. The slightest Italian accent. Utterly enigmatic.

She rolled onto her side so she didn't need to look at him.

'Us mortals have doctors too, you know, Raffa. I was managing perfectly well with my own antenatal appointments.'

'I've printed some of the scans of the *bambino*,' he said, ignoring her. 'It makes it all seem even more real.'

She knew exactly what he meant. The last scan she had seen had been weeks and weeks earlier. A tiny bundle—all head and little limbs. Today's scan was incredibly clear and in colour—every detail somehow conveying the proud, quiet dignity of their baby boy. There was no doubt he looked like his father. But she wasn't going to acknowledge that to him. The less she could share with him the better. They weren't some happy little family, cooing over their growing baby together. They were at war, no matter how he tried to dress it up.

She stared through the panes of glass to the bare branches of the trees that screened the house from the road. Trees that children could climb...

'Did you grow up here?' she said suddenly. 'You and Salvatore?'

He paused.

'Not Salvatore, no. This house belonged to my mother. It was held in trust for me until I was twenty-one. We spent most of our time at the villa in Rome before I went to school, but Christmas was always here in London. Why do you ask?'

She sat up on her elbows, glanced over her shoulder to where he stood, framed in the doorway, exuding that magnetic *something* that drew her to swing her legs to the ground and move closer to him.

'It occurred to me that you might have been growing up

here while I was five miles away across town. And how different our lives must have been.'

She didn't mean to let bitterness glaze her words but it did, and the taste seeped into the air between them.

'I hear what you're saying. And I'm the first to admit that I had privilege, *cara*. But would I rather have had my own mother and father alive and live in poverty with them? Yes, I would.'

If he'd slapped her she couldn't have felt his reproach more sharply.

'I'm sorry. I never thought of it like that before. Of course you must have missed your own parents.'

'Every day.' His gaze flicked to the dressing table, as if he half expected to see his mother sitting there. But then he trained it back on her—relentless. 'Children need their parents just as parents need their children. They need to be there, to keep them safe and protect them. And it's unfair of anyone to get in the way of that.'

'I wasn't trying to keep you out, Raffa. I didn't think you'd want to know.'

'You never gave me the chance.'

He stared through every inch of her self-righteousness like a drill through concrete, splintering her excuses. But he was right.

She swallowed. 'I was going to tell you. Of course I was.'

'When? After the birth? When he started to walk? First day at school? How much of my son's life did you think it reasonable to deprive me of?'

She cringed. How had she failed so spectacularly to see things from his point of view? Why had she ignored the voice in her head that told her he had the right to know?

'It wasn't like that, Raffa. You threw me out! The Di Viscontis didn't want to know me my whole life and—'

He put his hand up.

'I'm not going to judge them. And I'm not going to fight with you about why we're here. That is a complete waste of my time and yours. The baby is well, thank God, and from here on in we focus on the future. So tell me what you need. Your mother—do you want a car sent for her?'

'No! Not yet.'

She shook her head vigorously and walked to the window. She couldn't let her mother know where she was. She had to think this through. The minute Lynda heard that she was with Raffa in Regent's Park she would start to imagine all sorts of fairytale nonsense. She'd start dreaming of engagements and weddings and christenings and one huge happily-ever-after.

Because that was what Lynda had wasted her entire life on—hoping Prince Charming would come for her.

And had that happened? *No.* Things like that didn't happen in real life. All this dust-free polished wood and these freshly laundered linens. This was the same make-believe world she'd been seduced by six months earlier, when she'd won over Raffaele and ignored Mariella. A world which had seemed about to open up like a flower in sunshine, only to shrink and shrivel and close.

She knew better now. Luck like that didn't land in your lap.

No. She couldn't risk her mother's fragile mental health taking another tumble until she knew herself which way was up. The doctor had taken DNA swabs and the results would be ready in twenty-four hours. Then there would be a discussion about the birth and then an arrangement for contact. And work. She *really* needed to get work— surely the job at MacIver was hers…?

'Very well. Then we'll head to Hydros immediately.'

Another order. She stared at his retreating back.

'Hydros? Why on earth would we want to go *there*? I don't want a holiday. I want a job.'

'We're not going on holiday,' he said, rapidly typing something into his phone before dropping it into his pocket.

Then he turned and stared at her, full beam.

'We're going away from here—out of sight of the press—to sort out private family business. That's how I deal with things. Remember?'

Suddenly Coral began to realise that she'd crossed the line. She was now part of his world. His micro-management of *la famiglia* Di Visconti now included *her*. Every move she made was now going to be second-guessed and scrutinised, risk-assessed and managed. If he'd thrown chains over her she wouldn't have felt any more trapped.

'We'll get the DNA results tomorrow and by then we'll have figured out how we're going to play things. Plus, Salvatore is heading to Hydros—so it makes sense to meet him there and get the other DNA test over with. It's either that or a trip to Sydney.'

Salvatore? Sydney? Agreeing to one paternity test was bad enough, but she had no need to prove anything to anyone.

'Hang on—hang on! This is all going far too fast, Raffa. I don't want to go anywhere near Salvatore. I get it that you want *your* test done. I accept that someone in your position needs to be sure that I'm not some crazy person trying to stick it to you. And I get that you don't want this splashed over the front pages. But I've already told you I don't give a damn about proving that I'm a Di Visconti to anyone. I'm more than happy as a Dahl.'

'Don't be so naïve, Coral. You can't honestly have thought things were going to stay the way they were? You're Giancarlo Di Visconti's *daughter*, for God's sake. Waitressing isn't an option. And now you're pregnant?

Forget it. Anyway, I was never going to leave things as they were. It was wrong. What happened to your mother was wrong. I know about her debts. I know about your upbringing. All of it. I'm surprised that you don't want to put things right. There's more than you to consider in this.'

'Actually, there's *only* me to consider in this. And I've considered it. They didn't want me. And—guess what?— I don't want them.'

She knew the words sounded silly and petulant, but surely he saw it from her point of view?

Clearly he didn't. The look on his face said it all as his brilliant blue eyes bored into hers. *Selfish*. He thought she was being inconsiderate, depriving his baby of an even bigger fortune from the precious Di Viscontis.

'I've told you that I'm not going to argue with you. We've both made mistakes. But this is real. These are big issues and you can't take cover behind a coffee machine or a camera. You've got responsibilities now. That child deserves what you never had.'

He walked away, his ever-steady voice now rising, anger thrumming through every syllable.

Damn him. He was making her feel that she was already failing her son.

'You don't need money to have a happy childhood,' she said shrilly.

He was halfway along the hallway. He stopped at the top of the stairs and turned, one hand on the gleaming banister. Light flooded in from the glass cupola in the ceiling, down on the walls hung with oil paintings of haughty, beautiful women and plump-cheeked cherubic children.

For a fleeting moment she wondered if they were his ancestors, and if her child would look like them.

'Agreed! Children need parents. Two of them. Which he has—thank God.'

He checked his watch, hitched an eyebrow, smiled without mirth.

'We'll leave in an hour. Are you ready?'

He started down the stairs without waiting for her reply. She felt she'd been judged and sentenced and now she was going to be put in detention. Like a silly little girl let loose with a big bag of sweeties, keeping them all for herself and not thinking about the consequences.

'No, I'm *not* ready! There are other things I need to sort out first,' she said, hurrying after him.

'Such as?' he said, walking straight past the vases of perfectly poised lilies like a king past his courtiers.

'Like my work. Am I just supposed to forget about that now? And what about the MacIver job? Is it mine or isn't it?'

He turned into an office. A polished oak table stretched all the way up the centre of the room, behind which hung four large screens and four clocks, showing the time in New York, Sydney, Paris and Rome. He walked to a desk and lifted a tablet from underneath a folder. She could see a print-out of the baby's scan photograph through the clear plastic cover.

'I'm not going to complicate things further by employing you. Here—take this.'

He typed into the tablet and held it out. She could see the home page of one of the most exclusive boutiques in London.

'We've got some time before we fly. Why don't you choose some proper maternity clothes? They can be delivered to Hydros.'

She snatched the tablet, switched off the screen and shoved it down on the table. It rattled as it landed, but finally he was looking at her.

'Sorry if I'm not being clear. No, I'm *not* going to pick

out some *"proper"* clothes. Let me say it again: I'm only here with you because of these tests. As soon as they are confirmed I'm going back to my own life. In my own clothes. And if you're going to play God by refusing to give me that job at MacIver, then I'll keep on waitressing. I don't need your charity.'

That was a lie. She knew it and he knew it. There was no photography work falling into her lap, and she was too pregnant for waitressing. Soon she'd have nowhere left to turn unless it was to state benefits. Or Salvatore—and *that* was never going to happen.

He closed the space between them, stepping towards her like a challenge. She stood her ground, heart pounding, chest heaving and blood rushing in her ears.

'You're not getting my charity. You're getting my care. Whether you like it or not.'

His lips parted as he slowly stated each word. His eyes flashed all over her face, then landed on her mouth. They stared at one another, for one long moment and then another. Then, with just the slant of an eyebrow, he seemed to slash through the fractious, angry air and it suddenly settled into something much, much heavier.

'But you *do* like it, don't you? As I recall, you like it very much.'

She stared at his broad, muscled chest under the light cashmere sweater, at the perfect dark curve of his beard where it met his neck. She stared at the outline of his biceps and shoulders, his protector's body. She breathed in his strength and his pure male magnetism.

When she looked up into his face she knew she should hate him. She should despise those brilliant eyes and scorn his perfect lips. She should turn her face away, grab the reins of her life back and gallop for the hills. But she couldn't. She was rooted to the spot, drinking him in.

'You'll need to stop fighting me, *cara*. Sooner or later.' His tone softened. He closed the last inches between them. 'It won't all be bad. We've got something special—you can't possibly deny that.'

She felt his fingers closing around hers as he tugged her towards him.

'Remember how good it was when you stopped fighting me before? Remember…?'

His voice was barely a whisper now, his breath close to her ear. Her body erupted with lust as he shifted even closer.

'Remember how you begged me to take you?'

Yes! screamed her hot, aching body. *Yes!*

He lifted his fingers to her cheek. He slid his hand to her jaw. He bent forward one tiny fraction, then another, and another. Her eyes darted to his lips. He was going to kiss her.

She hovered for a moment, once more torn between following her head and following her heart, but she could no more stop the wave of longing that washed over her than stop breathing.

She closed her eyes and gave in.

And then he kissed her.

He pressed his lips to hers and she felt the rasp of beard, the firm demand of one kiss, then another. She smelled his cologne and a trace of espresso. She opened her mouth to his tongue's darting and probing and pushed her own tongue back as they met one another in a hunger she could barely contain.

She grabbed at his sweater and he held her wrists.

'Not here—not in my office,' he panted.

His eyes were dark as the night sky, and it made her almost cry out to know she affected him so deeply.

'*Yes*, here,' she said, looking at the wide expanse of polished walnut.

She could barely speak, so desperate was she to feel his flesh, fill her hands with him and satisfy the need that had built since that night.

She tried to draw him back to her.

'No,' he said, pulling away and shaking his head softly. 'We'll go upstairs. We'll take our time. Let me look after you. Please, Coral. Let me start to look after you now.'

CHAPTER NINE

HE GRASPED HER hand and tucked her underneath his shoulder. Without a single sound he walked her out of the office, along the hallway to the stairs. He was not going to give her a moment to change her mind because finally—finally—she had stopped combatting every single thing he said. Finally she was relenting.

But he knew her fire. She was exactly like her father. All it would take was one wrong word and she'd be stripping off her dress and stamping it into the ground again.

He kept her close, taking each step with her. He shouldn't have had to seduce her to get her to calm down, but the fire in his blood was out of control just as before. At least this way they would both get what they needed.

Round the twist in the stairs she almost stumbled, and he caught her swiftly. But even that made him stop, turn her in his arms, cup her beautiful face and kiss her sweet mouth. God, but he could not stop kissing her.

He wrapped his arms around her and pulled her tight to his body. It killed him to think of what she had been through. What had Giancarlo been *thinking*? How could he have shut out his own flesh and blood? There was nothing more important than family. *Nothing*.

And here he was, holding her tight and squeezing his promises into her. Here in his mother's house, under paintings of his great-grandmother and her sisters, and their children. *Family.* Never before had he felt the responsibility of all those generations as keenly as he did now.

I'm going to be a father, he told them all, pausing for a moment to feel them in the empty air. *I won't let you down,* he said, tears burning behind his eyes. *I will do my best to make you proud.*

His jaw clenched where it lay on her head, and his muscles tensed all around her. Around his child.

He knew it was his in his bones. Had known it since she'd thrown out her claim in that office. Yes, it was his child. And *she* was his woman.

She moved against him and he stiffened. Nothing could stop him from taking her to his bed now.

In seconds they were inside his suite. He closed the door. She was standing halfway across the floor, the apples of her cheeks as red as her tunic, her magnificent auburn hair ready to tumble down her naked shoulders.

'What are you waiting for?' she said. 'You don't need to be gentle.'

Her eyes were wild and her lips moist. In a single step he grabbed her and thrust his tongue into her mouth. She whimpered.

'Don't try to order me around,' he warned her, pausing for a second to cup her jaw with one hand and her breast with the other. Then he felt for her nipple and rolled it between his thumb and forefinger.

She gasped and pressed her hand on top of his. 'Don't stop. Please!' she cried.

'I've no intention of stopping,' he said, tugging her face to meet his and laving her mouth with his tongue. His hands moulded her fabulous heavy breasts, so full he could barely contain them. He wanted to see her—see how she had changed with the baby.

She was as greedy as he remembered, and in moments he felt her hands fumbling with his flies. She unbuttoned him as he continued to swell and grow. Then she worked her fingers inside his shorts until she had released him into her hand.

He stopped then. He had to see—had to imprint this on his mind for ever. The sight of him, hard and hot, in her hand. He looked into her face as she hitched her head back with pride and control and he felt the balance shift. She was his equal. And the fire in his blood raged harder.

Then she clasped him in her hand and worked it up and down, her clever fingers rubbing perfectly on his most sensitive area. He groaned his pleasure, feeling the intensity build below the head.

'Coral—please.'

She eyed him steadily, then bent to take him in her mouth. But he couldn't let her. 'Sweetheart.'

He scooped her up and sat her on the bed. Then he stripped off his sweater and trousers and everything else.

Her eyes widened and her mouth opened, breathing out a gasp. 'Oh!'

He stood with legs apart in front of her, his erection full and hard at ninety degrees to his body, inches away from her mouth.

She licked her lips. He leant behind her and unzipped her tunic, but she tugged him into her mouth and worked her tongue around him. It was warm and wet and so, *so* good.

But he stopped, stepped back. She was still clothed and he wanted every last piece of perfection spread out before him. He was going to give her what she needed.

In seconds he had pulled off her tunic and unfastened her bra. Her breasts fell into his hands and he bent his head to kiss the heavy white flesh and lick her erect rosy nipples.

Again she cried out when he touched them.

'Angel...' he said, easing her back, but still she held his head to them and he nuzzled against her, scenting her, glorying in her.

Gently he laid her back to tug off her other clothes, and he marvelled in the lush, feminine woman she had become. Her hair fanned out like a halo, her body round and flowing like life itself.

Finally he found what he wanted—the dark dart of hair at the apex of her thighs, shielding her soft, moist lips and her tiny hard pearl.

He took her knees in his hands and spread her legs, loving how her flesh opened for him. Then he settled down on his knees and did what he had longed to do all this time. He tasted her, working his tongue against her most sensitive area. He kissed and sucked and licked her until he had truly learned her deepest most womanly essence.

He looked up as she lifted her head. Her eyes were glazed with pleasure, but she speared him with a long look and in it he saw hope and fear and trust.

He clutched her hips and worked at her, hearing her call his name, urging him on. He flicked his tongue over and over her hot, hard bud, now swollen and bursting, ready to throb with her orgasm. Then he felt her hips rise up in the air and he suckled her hard. She screamed and released and broke apart for him. And it was beautiful.

In a heartbeat he was on his feet, cradling her, rolling her gently onto her side. Then, as he held her breasts in his hands, he slid his aching cock inside her. Her hands reached around him, grabbing him and urging him on, still crying out her pleasure. With every thrust he kept her going. He knew he was only moments behind her. He felt his own release build, and finally he pulsed and poured himself into her—over and over again.

Moments passed. More moments. Their breath slowed and heat began to grow between their bodies. Usually he could never hold a woman close after lovemaking, but he held her tight, relishing what they'd done. It had been immense. Amazing. It was incredible how sex was so different with her. Like taming a tiger, coaxing her to trust him. That feeling as she'd looked into his eyes had meant more to him than all the declarations of love he'd heard over the years from other women.

He placed his hands on her stomach gently, reverently. He smoothed his fingers over her skin, lightly probing the precious bundle she contained.

'He's fine in there?' he asked.

He felt her shift away from him.

'Of course.'

She disentangled her arms from his and pulled the sheet between them, tucking herself further away.

'Is everything OK?'

She shifted further, swung her legs onto the floor and stood up.

'Yes, I'm fine,' she said, but she didn't turn around.

He sat up on one elbow, watching as she walked into the en suite bathroom, more perfect than the Venus de Milo. His own goddess, come to life.

'I'm going to shower,' she said, and closed the door.

Raffaele lay back, spread his arms wide and pushed a pillow behind his head, running what they'd done through his mind, comparing it to the first time, when he'd taken her in the shower. He should have gone slow and steady. They'd need to work their way up to that, he thought, smiling to himself.

He was getting hard again, even thinking about it. He put his hand on his cock and stroked. Yes. Hydros could wait another half-hour.

He walked to the door of the bathroom. The shower was on. He knocked and entered. But instead of his beautiful goddess, soaked with suds and wet with desire, he saw she was leaning on outstretched arms over the sink, staring at herself in the mirror.

She turned sharply. 'I'm fine. I won't be long,' she said, fixing him with that haughty look.

He hung around the doorframe, trying to figure out what was happening, but she didn't move away from the sink.

'Do you feel sick? Is that what's wrong?'

Clearly something was up. He stepped forward to pull her into his arms, but she grabbed up a towel like a matador and skirted away, opening the shower door, stepping inside and flicking the towel over the glass in one smooth movement.

'I'm perfectly fine, thanks,' she said, closing the screen and turning away from him. She lifted her face to the spray and then stood, washing the droplets from her cheeks.

He watched her for a few more moments. This was not a woman who wanted more sex, that was for certain. But that was the only thing that was certain. Because he could not understand how she could have been screaming his name, begging him to fill her, giving him that look, with those eyes that told him she was *there* with him in those moments. He hadn't imagined any of that. And now she was as cold and distant and hostile as a Martian winter.

How had that happened?

It was moments like this that really pounded him in the gut. He didn't understand women. But, then again, how could he? His childhood had been spent in boarding school or on holiday, dodging Salvatore's emotional bullets. The few years he'd had with his mother had been shared with a nanny, basking in her sunshine only when she stopped filming for a moment.

But those rare moments had lit him up. When his *mamma* had hugged him close and kissed him he'd buried his face in her neck and felt flooded with love. It didn't matter that she'd only been there in fleeting moments. She'd been his *mamma* and he her darling and there had been nothing in the world that would come between them.

And then she'd gone. Her life snuffed out in seconds. Wrenched from him for ever. Taking with her a piece of his heart he'd never get back.

The time had passed when the pain of not being able to reach out and touch her or hear her voice had almost made life not worth living. When the braying torments of Salvatore had forced him to hide with his comics under the bed, where he'd silently sob himself to sleep.

Those days had gone. The pain was easier to bear, but, God, how he missed what they might have been. She would have helped him with so much. Now, here, with Coral. She would have shown him how to navigate these waters, because he was way out of his depth with this one.

All he knew for sure was that he would look after Coral. She didn't know how fragile life was. But he would keep her safe. Even if she fought him. Even if she chose to reject him while she stood there like marble under a waterfall— only a little more rocklike. A little more impenetrable.

Coral grabbed at the shampoo and squeezed it angrily into her hand. As she lathered up she saw him turn and walk away.

Good. Go away, she thought, furiously rubbing the foam into her head, feeling it soak through her fingers and down her back. *Take your irresistible body and your picture-perfect face and your mouthwatering maleness and leave me alone.*

Shampoo soaked into her eyes, stinging them. Furiously, she rubbed and splashed them with water.

Why on earth had she let that happen? Why had she let herself believe that he cared when all he was doing was scratching an itch and keeping her sweet because she was carrying his child. For one moment she had actually thought he might really care for her. He'd seemed genuinely interested in giving her pleasure.

He had given her the best orgasm of her life.

She stood still now under the shower, remembering as water coursed down her face and shoulders. What had he done to her? He had ruined her for ever for other men. Nothing would ever be the same again. It had been bad enough the first time. But she'd almost managed to forget what she'd felt and unlearn what he'd taught her about herself. *Almost* managed, while she'd been stuck in Islington with the publishing world's doors closing in her face, no money in her purse and morning sickness that almost felled her daily.

But not now. Now it was imprinted on every nerve in her body that her son's father was her ultimate fantasy come to life. And she'd have her own mini-Raffaele there to remind her of that for evermore.

She turned off the taps and grabbed at the towel. This anger was hers to own. She was responsible for getting herself into this situation not once but twice. She had allowed her physical desire for him to trump every last grain of common sense she had and *knowingly* and *willingly* had sex with him.

And beautifully.

And wonderfully.

She sighed, clutched the towel against her body and pushed out of the shower. She opened the door an inch to check if he was there. No sign. Of course not. Why would he be waiting there for her? Men cared only about sex, not intimacy. They cared about physical pleasure, not emotional commitment.

He hadn't rolled her over and asked how she was feeling after they'd had sex. He couldn't care less that she had opened herself up and laid herself bare. He'd patted her stomach to make sure the baby was OK, then followed her into the bathroom with his erection twitching for more.

She padded across the rug, her feet sinking into the velvety pile. As expected, there was no sign of anything other than her crumpled red tunic and worn-out boots lying beside the puddle of silk sheets like so much rubbish dropped in the snow.

'Get yourself some proper maternity clothes.'

She looked at her charity shop finds. Maybe she damn well would. Maybe she'd stop playing the martyr and get back in the saddle of her own life. Six months ago she'd been a different person. She'd been pushing ahead, her face turned towards the sun. *That* Coral wouldn't have let herself be treated like some temporary sex toy. *That* Coral was out there cutting her path, not hiding behind her pregnancy, begging for a job.

She picked up the tunic and held it out. Was she *really* going to continue to dress herself in rags and trundle about on public transport while her half-brother and the father of her child dressed in silk and cashmere and were ferried around in private jets and yachts? What kind of fool did that?

Not this one. Not any more.

She sat on the bed and stared around.

This stopped now.

If she was a part of this world then she was going to be a full part. Not some supporting actress who stepped in for a sex scene and then waited in the wings while the men forged forward with their lives.

She had an unclaimed fortune…

She was in the middle of one of the most beautiful houses in Regent's Park…

It was a Rossini house, but the Di Viscontis had houses all over the world too. *And* a fleet of cruise ships. Those were just the parts she knew about. She might have missed out on their wonderful world, but there was no way she would deny her son all the things she'd never had. She wanted to make him proud of her—of course she did. And that started with giving him somewhere to live that was warm and happy and safe.

Somewhere like this.

All around her the antique furniture of the Rossini family bore witness. How many other women had been in these rooms over the years and generations? She'd bet each elegant piece had seen its fair share of happiness and pain, marriage and divorce…

Raffa might be saying all the right things now, but how long would that last? How could she be sure he wouldn't tire of her and the baby?

Suddenly she felt a sharp stab of pain—an echo of what her mother had been through, pining for her love and sheltering her child. How many times had she contacted Giancarlo, pleading for him to come back to her?

Coral shuddered and pulled the damp towel around her. She wasn't going to allow that to happen. She wasn't going to allow any man to hold the keys to her happiness. Because she could be sure of nothing in this world other than the fact that there was no one at her back and there never would be. Whatever she achieved in this world was down to her.

So maybe it was time that she stopped playing the pride card.

She looked around for the tablet. It must be in the office.

She put on a robe and hurried downstairs.

* * *

At the back of the house, behind the kitchens, a short flight of wooden steps led down to the basement. Raffaele stood there now, gazing down into the half-light, absorbing the familiar waft of dry air and the scents that marked out the laundry and stores of dry goods.

If he let his eyes glaze he could almost see the dogs in the corner by the door to the wine cellar. He could almost sense his father tinkering about, choosing wine for dinner, beckoning him closer, holding a bottle of vintage red covered in dust up to his nose and then blowing. Laughing as the cloudy puff settled in the air, on father and son together.

Memories like those were precious, rubbed from his mind like a genie from a lamp, but so fleeting and fragile. The harder he tried to grab at them the more quickly they disappeared.

He moved down each creaking step and into the depths of the cellar, going towards the safe room. Most of the jewellery was still here. Kept intact with everything else in the house, even the staff, as if they were waiting for the moment when the family would be back again.

And now it would. He could almost feel the past reshaping itself. It was going to happen. It was as if all those years of dark pain might now be eclipsed by some light, some happy symmetry, where he might once again taste the fruit of a real family.

He opened the safe and pulled out a box, finding immediately what he was looking for. His grandmother's engagement ring. The ring he had pictured on Coral's finger the moment he had known he was going to ask her to marry him. He held it between his finger and thumb and it caught flashes of light, even there in the cellar's gloom.

Yes, it was such an obvious solution—and it would solve

her anxieties in one moment. It was the only thing that made sense. It would give her the security she needed.

That *had* to be the reason she was acting out. She wasn't angry with him—she was afraid. Afraid of being alone because Giancarlo hadn't married her mother and hadn't even *tried* to have a relationship with her. In her mind she'd been rejected and abandoned, so she was doing what all abandoned children did so well—keeping people back, because they'd only go and leave anyway. Didn't he know that better than anyone? *Never let people get close.* But Coral didn't have the benefit of several years of therapy to reach that conclusion herself.

So he would marry her and keep them all safe. The Rossini family and the Di Visconti family would be aligned. He would right Giancarlo's wrongs and give Coral the life she had missed out on. Salvatore would be enraged—but wasn't he always? And they would need nothing from him. Romano's net worth was already half as much again as Argento's. And in a few years Raffaele would be able to step away from babysitting the cruise ships.

It was almost too perfect—and it was all within his grasp.

He slipped the ring into his pocket.

He would ask her tomorrow night at dinner. Before Salvatore arrived and had to be managed into handing over a DNA sample.

He crushed his hand round the little velvet box.

Yes, this was the way. The only way. It felt good. It felt right. Like when he'd left Rome to go to New York and when he'd launched *Heavenly*. When things felt like this it eased the knot in his stomach—for a little while, at least.

CHAPTER TEN

THIS DINNER WAS not going well. Everything was wrong. Coral had dropped her knife and knocked over her glass. She'd spilled soup down her dress and almost singed her hair on a candle. Raffa sat inches away from her, the strong angles of his face licked by the candles' golden glow, his steady gaze assessing her without a flicker of emotion.

'You seem a little anxious. Is everything all right?' he asked.

She dabbed her napkin at a new stain on her lap.

'I'm fine. It's fine,' she lied.

She was far from fine. No matter how hard she tried she couldn't rein in her emotions. The more composed and relaxed he got, the more vexed she felt.

In the little time they'd spent together since they'd left for the island he'd seemed to increase the easy charm as she became more and more waspish.

As soon as the plane had landed on Hydros she'd shot off with her camera, down to the little harbour, losing herself in images of rocky islands rearing up in the background and sea-battered driftwood in the stony foreground.

Usually her art gave her the space she needed to work out her thoughts, but her head had still been a mess. She hadn't been able to help but think that the last time she'd viewed this horizon her head had been full of wonder and promise, stealing images from someone else's world. But this time she was looking out at a vista that was slowly taking on a new meaning. It was a vista her father had enjoyed. A vista her son would enjoy.

She'd looked along the bay, imagining him playing in the sand, and felt suddenly how *right* that was. He should have everything in this world that would make him happy, despite how it made her feel.

When Raffa's call had come, saying that the DNA test was a positive match she'd barely registered it. Of *course* it was. She'd made her way back to the new house with a clutch of beautiful images and a promise to herself to stop being so passive. She was going to get some advice. Some proper legal advice to see what her options were.

Now she listened with awe as Raffa told the story of how far Romano Publishing had come in five short years. How he'd built up the core business and could now acquire loss-making brands like MacIver because of their creativity and industry stature.

He spoke of how he'd started *Heavenly*. The risks he'd taken, the hours he'd worked until it had finally paid off. Not just financially, but by reputation. He knew everyone and everyone knew him.

He was out there in the world cutting a path, doing amazing, unforgettable things. And she wasn't.

No matter how he dressed it up, he was following his dreams and she still wasn't even being given the chance. That was wrong. But she couldn't seem to hate him for it.

Not when every nerve danced to his tune, when every sense was alive to his nearness and the thought of his touch made her weak-kneed and desperate.

'You don't have much of an appetite?' he said now.

She glanced at their respective plates—his clear and hers cluttered.

'I'm not very hungry.'

'Are you queasy? I should have thought. I'm sorry, that was inconsiderate.'

He reached his hand across and lifted her fingers. She stared wide-eyed at the gesture—at her fingers in his. They'd done something so much more intimate than hand-holding the day before.

She yanked them away. 'No, I'm fine. Past all that. I wasn't great for the first few months, but I feel better than ever now. Full of good health, actually. I could take on the world.'

As soon as she got out there.

He nodded, watching her. 'You do look incredible. I'd never properly appreciated what was meant by the "bloom" of pregnancy before. But everything about you—your hair, your skin—is glowing. It's amazing.'

He reached across and lifted a handful of her hair. She felt the brush of his fingers on her neck and the wildfire of lust spread through her body. She inhaled sharply, gripping the edge of her chair. She mustn't let him see how he affected her. She had to stay on track.

'The moment I saw you step off the jet I knew I wanted to touch this hair. Feel it in my hands.'

She turned her face and pulled her head away, and he slowly let her hair slide through his fingers.

He sat back again in his chair. Lifted his glass, sipped a little water. 'You took my breath away, Coral. You still do.'

'You took mine away when you threw me off this island,' she said, turning to look at him.

It still burned and she wouldn't forgive him so easily.

Slowly he replaced the glass on the table. 'I'll regret that moment for ever. But we are amazing lovers. You must admit if it hadn't been for circumstances we'd have had a very good chance of making a proper go of things.'

'Circumstances which you're just about to reintroduce. I don't need any kind of reconciliation with Salvatore to know that he's my half-brother.'

'As soon as we get a DNA sample from him we can start to put the rest of our lives in order,' he said, not taking the bait.

Nothing seemed to induce him to retaliate.

'I was putting my life in order before I met you, Raffa. I was starting my career. And I'll be doing so again. That's not up for debate.'

He smiled and leaned further back, putting his hands on the table in a gesture of openness. She looked at the breadth of his palms, at his fingers splayed wide. Lover's hands. Protector's hands. Chairman of the Board's hands.

'I want the best for you. You're going to be the mother of my child. I will look after you. It's the right thing to do.'

'I don't need a man to look after me. I wasn't brought up that way.'

She felt her anger return, felt her spine straighten. She wasn't going to rely on any man for her happiness. She was independent, and that wasn't going to change just because she was going to have Raffaele Rossini's baby.

He nodded. 'I know. It was unforgivable, what happened to you. And it is something we will work through together. Whatever it takes, I promise. But tonight, Coral, let's just be *us* again. Let's properly learn to know one another.'

'What is there that you don't already know, Raffa? I won't be steamrollered by you. I'm too independent. And having a baby with you isn't going to change that. If anything, it's made me feel even more determined. I'm going to be a working single mother. It's no big deal. It's been done before—loads of times.'

He raised an eyebrow and fixed her with his bright blue

gaze. She should look away indignantly. But she couldn't. She found herself staring back, ensnared by the brilliance.

'No one will ever treat you better than I will. No one will care for you and keep you safe.'

He sat up and reached for her hands. She felt herself deliver them over to him.

'I want us to be married, Coral. In fact, I can't think of anything I want more.'

'Married?' she gasped. *'Married?'*

'Indeed. A marriage contract. Rossini and Di Visconti. The two families should be aligned in law. It's the right thing to do, Coral.'

His gaze never wavered as he slipped one hand below the table for a moment and then produced a ring. A beautiful square-cut yellow diamond, flanked by two clear stones. Its brilliance and beauty stunned her.

Her eyes dropped as he slid the ring on her finger.

'In one move we will sort this whole thing out. You. Our son. Me. It's the only possible way forward.'

She stared at the beautiful ring on her hand. Her heart thudded in her chest. He was asking her to marry him— but not in the way every girl dreamed it would happen. She had hoped that one day a prince would come for her, just as her mother had said. A prince who would fall on his knees and confess that he wanted to live with her and her alone. Who would promise to cherish her and share his world with her. Only her, and only because of their love.

Raffaele was proposing a contract. Because she was part of *la famiglia*—just another commodity to be guarded. It was business—*family* business—and the only two families that counted were the Di Viscontis and the Rossinis.

A contract.

But contracts could be broken.

Marriages could be annulled.

The underground stream whispered by. The chandelier swayed slightly. Over Raffaele's shoulder a light blinked out on the rolling sea. Once, twice. Her eyes flickered. She felt as alone and vulnerable as that solitary boat.

He drew her fingers to his lips and kissed them.

'Sleep on it, *cara*.'

CHAPTER ELEVEN

RAFFA SCRAPED BACK his chair and went out onto the terrace, filling his lungs with the fresh clean air and gazing up at the inky black sky that he desperately hoped would give him some perspective on what had just happened.

He took the steps two at a time and struck off along the path, the dogs at his heel. The moon was huge and bare of clouds, and the path to the bay was etched out for him as clearly as it was in his memory.

He reached the rocks and vaulted them easily, trotting onto the sand. The tide was out and he jogged onto hard-packed sand, feeling the tension slip away as each passing wave rolled up to his trousers and shoes, soaking them.

How could he have called it so badly wrong? He'd been so *sure* that this was the right way. The *only* way. Was she really so against it? Or was it just her way always to be so damned difficult? Didn't she know that asking her to marry him was the biggest thing he had ever done in his life? It was the ultimate decision and he had chosen *her*. Out of all those women who had flung themselves at him over the years, *she* was the one.

The look on her face had been one of horror, not joy, and that hurt him. It did. She was the mother of his child. All that talk of being an independent single mother... There was no need for that. They should be *together*, for God's sake. He had already known the baby was his, but hearing the results had cemented his resolve to do the very best for them all. He would not permit anything to go wrong.

He had fully expected that as the baby's mother she would want to be with him too. She had to feel their chemistry the same way he did. It bubbled under the surface of every exchange they had. They were explosive together. He ached for her. He'd pleasured himself thinking about her all those weeks when he'd tried to forget her. *Her*. Only her.

Damn, but this was an impossible situation!

She couldn't *really* think there was going to be another way, could she? That he would get the test results then fire up the jet and drop her back in London to take orders for tea and coffee? And, when the *bambino* was born, did she *really* think that he would agree to have contact every other weekend? While she lived God knew where and did God knew what. With God knew whom…

Their son was heir to a global business—Romano Publishing. He had to learn about his world from birth, from his father. He had to know about his family and his responsibilities. He had to have everything he would need to grow up happy and healthy. And safe.

How could he look after his son if he wasn't fully part of his world? It was insane. It was not going to happen. He would have to make her see sense, one way or another.

He turned around to face the house. Lamps had been dimmed along its length, leaving only the kitchen and his suite lit. He stood as the sea rolled in its might behind his back, watching. Finally all the lights were extinguished and the house was in darkness.

Everything was as it should be.

Coral was where she should be.

He hadn't imagined for a moment that she would reject him, but he should have realised that a woman like her wasn't going to roll over. She'd proved that spectacularly enough already. He was going to have to be much more careful or she might reject him outright. And that was a situation he was not prepared to endure for a single moment.

He checked his phone. Twelve-thirty. He had a satellite meeting with his west coast team in half an hour, and briefings scheduled with the Argento office in Shanghai. Then he would catch some sleep for an hour or two.

After that he'd figure out his next move with Coral...

By the time he was finished working, daylight's grey-blue tones were spreading all through the house. The staff were already busy going about their tasks. The world was slowly waking up to a typical Adriatic December day. He hadn't slept, he needed coffee, and he hadn't cleared his head. Salvatore would be landing in a few hours and *that* situation was going to take a lot of skill to manage.

He opened the dining room door, bleary-eyed, looking for the coffee pot and at least a half-hour of solitary meditation. He needed this time every day—watching the sun rise and the birds wake up, the tide's ebb and flow. No matter where he was in the world, he needed this time. It stilled his mind, gave him perspective. He'd always treasured these moments alone even as a child—before Salvatore woke up and started needling him.

But there, sitting at the head of the table, framed by the gauzy seascape, sat Coral.

She dabbed her mouth with a napkin and set it down on the table. 'Good morning. Sleep well?'

He frowned and walked towards the coffee pot. 'Fine, thanks. And you?'

'Really well, thanks. I woke with such an appetite.'

'Well, you must make yourself at home. Have what you want.'

He poured a long coffee, never taking his eyes from her as she lifted cutlery and started to eat what seemed to be a full English breakfast with eggs and bacon.

'Oh, I have already, thanks. Chef's been great. We had a chat and he managed to produce this. He says he's delighted to have something more to do of a morning than heat up your porridge.'

'Is that right?' he said, slowly pacing towards her with his cup. She was seated on his chair, so he pulled out another and sat.

'Shall I tell him you're ready for it now?'

'No, I have a couple of these before I eat. But thank you.'

She smiled, then forked up a piece of egg and began to eat again. 'No problem.'

For a few moments he watched her, mesmerised, trying to figure out what was going on. She looked utterly radiant, with no trace of the anxiety he'd seen last night. She was wearing a dressing gown—*his* dressing gown—and it looked like a mink coat around her shoulders. Her skin was perfect—she glowed with health.

He stared at her as if she was a work of art.

'When do you want to talk about the wedding?' she said, suddenly.

The coffee caught in his throat and he spluttered a startled response. 'What?'

'The wedding?' she said, calmly continuing to eat her breakfast. 'You wanted my answer today.'

She put down the cutlery and stared at him. Yellow flashed at him. She was wearing the ring.

'Let's not waste any more time, Raffaele. The wedding—I've decided it's on. But the choices of venue are a bit limited, due to my condition, and time's marching on. I think your house in Rome would be fine, and it's not too far for my mother and my friends to travel there. I'm not so bothered about the rest of the guest list. I suppose there are people you'll need to invite. You can sort that. But I won't get married without my mother. As for the dress— off the peg is fine. I've shortlisted a few that I can check out when we get back to London.'

She placed her cup down with a sigh of contentment and pushed herself back from the table.

'Then there's you, of course. I know you'll not want to lose your place on the Best Dressed List, so I'm quite happy to leave you to choose your own clothes. The menu is all sorted—Chef and I have already discussed it—and we'll go with a very simple theme for the decorations. Probably unimaginative white. We don't want to raise any expectations.'

'Expectations?' he heard himself say stupidly.

'You know—that this is a big romantic moment. Though I suppose we'll need *some* sort of party...' she said, almost absentmindedly.

'A party—' he began, but instantly she interrupted.

'Getting a photographer might be tricky. But Mariella says she's sure she can get Markowitz. He's your favourite, isn't he?'

'You've been in touch with Mariella? What did you say?'

She'd turned to stare out at the birds that had already started to arrive in the garden. Her fingers coiled around a lock of glossy auburn hair—round and round she twisted it, hypnotically.

Then she turned to stare at him with a slight look of condescension. He'd never been condescended to in his entire life.

'What? We talked about the wedding, of course. Coverage will sell millions. "Wedding of the Year", as Mariella's already dubbed it. I'm thinking about selling the rights to the Hope Alliance, as they've helped Mum so much over the years with her mental health issues. I thought that was the right thing to do. Under the circumstances.'

'Just stop right there.'

She narrowed her eyes and leaned towards him.

'No, *you* stop right there! Before we go any further we'll work out the ground rules. Like, you don't *ever* talk to me like that. And stop assuming you can make decisions for me.'

A maid had come in. He heard her movements behind him. The coffee pot being replaced, lids on the serving dishes being opened and closed. Suddenly a bowl appeared in front of him.

'What is that?'

'Your porridge, of course. I thought you might like some fruit chopped up in it. Oatmeal alone is so dull.'

He pushed the bowl away.

'What is it you think you are doing here, Coral? Trying to irritate your way out of this?'

'On the contrary, Raffaele. My only interest now is securing the best possible terms and conditions for our contract. A businessman like you can surely understand that?'

Not for the first time he looked at her and saw her father. Shrewd, intelligent and determined. She was Giancarlo's daughter, all right. This could get…interesting.

'All right, Coral,' he said. 'I'm ready to listen. What is it you want?'

She sat back in the chair, placed her arms on the armrests and looked him square in the face. The yellow diamond sparkled traitorously on its new owner's finger.

'I've decided that you're right. Why am I fighting for the right to dress in second-hand clothes when I should have been enjoying this view all my life?'

She drew her hand in the air and looked out at the sea, her chin held high.

'So, yes, I have thought it through from every angle, Raffa. I could refuse your offer and go back to London. Whether or not we get married, morally you'd still have to put us up in a house, pay for staff and school fees. We'd share contact and do what loads of other couples do and everything would be fine. I know you'd do the right thing by us. I'm not saying that you'd stick around for ever—there are loads of dads who slip up when a shiny new family comes along—but I don't think you'd ever "do a Giancarlo", so to speak.'

She turned to face him. Her face was utterly calm, but her eyes were clouded with something that tugged at his heart.

'I thought I'd made that clear,' he said.

'You have. But I don't think you fully understand what you've offered. It's not just marriage, Raffa. It's bringing me face to face with a world I was never meant to see. All of this.'

She reached for her cup, laid her fingers around it as if for warmth.

'It's already cost me so much. Yesterday morning, down there on the beach, I looked around and all I saw were the ghosts of someone else's childhood. My father didn't want me because he had something better here.'

'I'm so sorry you feel like that, but it wasn't—' he began, but she shook her head.

'You don't know what it was like for me—what it *is* li—just as I don't know what you went through being orphaned. We're both damaged goods.'

Her eyes flicked from the cup to him and she delivered him a look layered with pain and shame and sorrow. A slight sad smile curled at her lips before she crushed them together.

'But I have to be optimistic. I have to assume that I'm not going to choke to death with jealousy every time I see a cruise ship or eat an olive. I'm not so bitter that I'm going to let it spoil the rest of my life. Because it's not really about me any more.'

She folded her napkin carefully and ran her finger along its edges, smoothing each crease. He got the sense that she was waiting for a reply—some sort of affirmation of her plan. He reached for her hand, gripped it, squeezing it in solidarity.

'No, you're right. It's got to be about our son.'

She didn't withdraw her hand for a moment, and he used the pause to rub little circles over the back of her hand, smoothing and soothing and trying to telegraph how much he wanted to care for her. But her head remained bowed and a deep, lonely sadness seemed to settle over her.

Finally she withdrew her hand and looked at him, a ghost of a smile on her face. 'That's what I thought. And that's what everything *must* be about from now on. We'll plan our lives around him. I'll be the best mother I can possibly be. And that includes being the best *person* I can be. So when I say that I want to work, it's because there's a creative part of me that I need to feed in order to feel whole. For him as well as me. Don't fight me on any of this, Raffa.'

'Of course not.'

When he looked now, the sadness was gone. Only the sure and steady certainty that he knew so well from her father remained.

'I'm not going to return to London to work in a café, or beg you for a job,' she cut in. 'I haven't figured everything out yet, Raffa. One thing at a time. But to be a good mother I need to be a whole person. I need my career.'

'I would never fight you on having a career. I'm as much

of a feminist as you are, *cara*. I'll support you in whatever you want to do.'

What they could achieve together would be immense, whether she stayed in photography or branched into other creative areas. She could hold court in any board meeting—it was surely only a matter of time before she realised that potential too.

He could feel the image forming more clearly. They would be a couple, a family, a little unit he'd protect and nurture. Coming home to each other, working together, spending time together, with all the fragments of his childhood blending to become his future.

Like a hot air balloon breaking free of its ties, his heart began to float upwards. Never before had he felt the grasp of joy so close at hand.

He looked at her. What an amazing woman… Every bit Giancarlo's daughter, but so much more. She had more courage than her father. She would have gone ahead with motherhood alone—done it all without him. She could have turned her back on him and he would not have found it in his heart to hate her for it. But she was giving them all a chance to be together. He could see that so clearly and it filled him with love.

He felt the rush of the words in his mouth, but he stopped himself. Never before had he used them. He wasn't afraid to say it, but he'd never found a woman he felt he could love. His mother had been his Madonna, and mortal women just didn't come close.

But Coral…

Strong, beautiful, courageous Coral.

She was surely the one woman in the world for him. And she was going to marry him. Grudgingly, and only for the sake of their son, but she was going to marry him.

He couldn't tell her that he loved her straight away. He

would have to be sure he didn't frighten her—or horrify her, the way he had when he'd proposed. Things were just beginning to fall into place. There was nothing to be gained from rash, emotional declarations now.

He steeled himself, reeling his feelings back in, closing them down and feeling reassuring self-containment descend upon him once again.

For a few moments the peaceful sounds of a couple breakfasting were all that could be heard, and that felt good. This was what it was going to be like. A normal, happy little family...

Then, with a whoosh of air, the maid opened the French doors just as the heavy throb of a jet's engines roared its arrival. It tore through the quiet morning and they both turned their faces upwards, watching for a moment as the plane circled and then began to land.

Salvatore.

Raffaele's buoyant heart sank with each hundred feet of the plane's descent.

'He's here already?' said Coral, turning to him, a look of resigned dread on her face.

'Looks like it,' he replied. 'It has to be done, Coral. Things will feel better when this last piece of the jigsaw is in place.'

'I hope you're right,' she said. 'But something tells me the grand family reunion might not turn out to be what I imagine.'

She stood then, and shook her hair in that lioness way she had. She smoothed her hands over her bump and only then did he notice a slight tremor. Her fingers were shaking. She was right on the edge. Dear God, but he so wanted to hold her, kiss her, love her the way his gut was telling him to.

'I'd better go and get ready. I'm twenty-five years late as it is.'

'Coral—' he said. But he spoke into the air.

She was already halfway to the door, thanking the maid warmly and then heading off down the hallway.

He turned and stared out through the open French doors, then in two strides made his way through them and out into the morning.

This was a meeting that was long overdue.

Once more he trotted down the cliffside path and along the curve of the bay to the old villa. The sky was clear and the morning brisk and fresh. His head was leaden with lack of sleep, but he knew that each step brought him closer to the end of his hurt and the beginning of his happiness.

The dogs trotted by his side, as they always did. Their ears were back—they felt the strain, too. Through the patchy scrub of the hedgerows a motorbike thundered past.

He felt the fist around his heart tighten.

He mounted the steps to the portico, clicked his fingers and the dogs dropped to the ground. But even as he entered he could feel the buzz of tension that Salvatore always carried with him.

The whole house was on edge. Staff scuttled past him, their eyes flicking him a smile but their heads bowed. He walked on through the hallway—past the Testinos and the ghosts of the fashion shoot.

He found him in the lounge, his face buried in his phone.

'*Ciao*, Salvatore.'

'What do you make of this place? Amateurs—all of them,' he said, barely glancing up. 'I fly two thousand miles and Chef isn't even here with my favourite dishes. He's at yours, I'm told. What's going on, Raffa? You don't normally pull rank.'

Raffaele walked in slowly, taking his place in the centre of the room.

'You were expected tonight. We arrived last night, so

Chef was with us. This morning I had fruit on my porridge. It made a pleasant change.'

'We? Us?' Salvatore said uninterestedly.

He threw himself down on the leather sofa and lay back, his dirty heels on the white calfskin—a pathetic little act of defiance against Giancarlo's rules. But he didn't raise his eyes, and for once Raffa let it slide.

'Anyway, I'm glad you're here early. I have news.'

'Yeah? Have you signed the business over to me? That's the only news I'm interested in.'

'I'm going to be a father.'

Salvatore's fingers stilled. Finally he looked up. The scowl over his eyes darkened. His mouth thinned, and then broke into a mocking smile.

'You are? Well, well... I must admit that was the last news I expected to hear. But, *bravo*. I take it you were as surprised as me? We can all be a little careless at times, I suppose. Who's the mummy? Anyone I know?'

Raffaele held his fury tight, like a ball of white-hot light in his hand.

'Actually, you do know her. You recall the photographer? Coral Dahl? The one you felt had delusions of being your half-sister? The one I threw off the island to please you?'

Salvatore's whole face blanched. Then his brows sank lower over his eyes. He swung his legs to the floor and stood. His hands formed into fists and Raffaele braced himself for combat.

But Salvatore was smarter than that. He turned his face and walked away. 'I can't believe this.'

'I need that issue to be resolved.'

'What issue?'

'The issue of her paternity. I need a swab or a blood sample from you, Salvatore. I'm sure you want to know the truth as much as I do.'

Gold-digging bitch—that had been the last thing Salvatore had called her when Raffaele had told him that he'd dealt with her that night. If Salvatore dared use the same language now he would rip his head off. But he didn't. He knew better.

Salvatore turned. Outside, the white trail of a speedboat tore a slice in the sea. Sunbeams settled into a carpet of white light across the water. The Adriatic winter was as peaceful as ever. But inside it was as if hell had spewed its thick air into the room.

They paced like two dogs braced to fight.

'You're *seriously* going to believe that scheming little opportunist against your own family? After all my father did for you? He would be *disgusted*, Raffa. If he'd wanted her to be in his life he would have brought her here! But he didn't. I can't believe you let your head be turned so easily. Just because she slept with you. And after all your lectures to *me*!'

'Careful what you say, Salvatore. Coral and I are having a child together. Regardless of what Giancarlo did, the fact remains that she is most probably your half-sister. So don't push me too far on this one, because you won't like where my sympathies lie.'

He forced himself not to move as Salvatore punched his own fist and then walked to the fireplace, his head buried in his hands. A wail came as if from deep in his stomach and it was hideous.

Then he turned and threw himself back down on the sofa. 'Raffa, I can't believe that *you*, of all people, are going to turn against me too. After everything I've been through. I thought you were the one person I could rely on.'

Salvatore sat sobbing, elbows on his knees and his head in his hands. He turned an anguished face to Raffa, flushed and garish.

'My life is in ruins. All those years of having to share Papa. Of never being good enough. Every day being compared to you, being told I must live up to you. Do you know how much I hated it when you came? Every single day was hellish for me—*hellish*.'

Raffaele swallowed. He knew this story. It was the best form of emotional blackmail and one that Salvatore always dished up when he felt cornered. But the worst thing about it was that it was true.

'Have you *any* idea how it feels to not even be given my own inheritance? To not be trusted with my own money? And now you're going to tell me there's someone else waiting to take my place. She's turned *you* against me, too.'

'It's not like that, Salvatore,' he began. 'This isn't about you. Coral has missed out on so much, but we're focussing on the future—not the past. Your inheritance is intact, and nothing will change between us.'

'How can you *say* that? Of *course* it will change. As soon as she gets her results she'll want a slice of Argento. Every single thing we've had as a family will be obliterated by her. Nothing will ever be the same again.'

Raffa watched the pitiful sight of Salvatore, his promise to Giancarlo churning in his mind. Of course he would never abandon him. He was weak. He needed support. But he was a grown man. Some day he had to learn to stand on his own two feet.

'Nothing will change. Coral isn't interested in Argento. She's a creative. She'll work with me at Romano. There's nothing for you to worry about, Salvatore.'

He said the words confidently, but unease gripped his throat. They'd not discussed anything properly, but she'd been dead against having anything to do with the Di Viscontis. Surely that included Argento?

Salvatore stood. He paced forward and reached out both

arms in the dramatic way he used when he wanted to drive
home a victory.

Raffa swallowed his distaste.

'Well, that's different. That's entirely different. Do you
promise, Raffa? That Argento will be mine?'

'I'm dealing with one thing at a time,' he said, with
Coral's words echoing in his ears. 'First the DNA sample.
Then I want you to come to say hello. Coral is expecting
us and I really want this to go well, Salvatore. There's a
hell of a lot riding on it.'

CHAPTER TWELVE

I COULD GET used to this, thought Coral, reclining in a chair as one maid worked on her hair while the other painted her toes. As they chatted happily in Greek, she heard more staff arriving, trundling rails of clothes into the dressing room to be unpacked.

The whole island was clearly delighted that Raffaele was back for a few days. He rarely came at this time of year, and it was a pleasure for them to see him. Of the whole family, he was clearly everyone's favourite.

Tell me something I don't know, she thought. *This whole thing would be so much easier if he wasn't.*

She opened her eyes and stared back at the woman in the mirror. Despite what she'd told Raffa she'd barely slept, tossing and turning all night, her mind still rammed with a thousand thoughts. Wondering if he would come to her… wondering what she would do if he did.

Her resolve not to be his temporary sex toy was now rendered completely moot. Their marriage would be consummated—of that there was no doubt. And she'd be a liar if she said she wasn't looking forward to that aspect of their union.

But what else about their marriage would be normal?

In the darkest hours, waves of self-pity had almost engulfed her. Here she was on her father's island—but not because he had ever wanted her here. Her father had never wanted her at all. It was as if she had gatecrashed his private world, despite all his efforts to keep her out.

And she was marrying the man almost every woman in publishing fantasised over. Why? Not because he loved her, but because she had trapped him. She had got herself pregnant and, because he was who he was, he'd stepped up and done 'the right thing'. Those were the words she could hear echoing round the publishing world.

Made a name for herself? She sure had.

But she had made her decision. Raffa had been right all along. It really didn't matter what anyone else thought. What mattered was securing her child's future. Raffa wanted marriage. And, try as she might, there was not a single fibre of her being that could deny that she wanted it too.

As she'd lain back in bed, staring at the ceiling, she'd allowed herself to imagine flashes of the days ahead. It was like dipping a spoon in honey, twirling it round and letting it drizzle down her throat, savouring its sweetness.

But she was a realist. That delicious future could disappear as quickly as it had come. There were no guarantees—no absolutes. So she would not sit back and let this all be on Raffa's terms. She would swallow her self-pity and find every single opportunity to gain her own independence.

Claiming her share of the Di Visconti inheritance was something she'd never have been able to do for herself. Her pride wouldn't have let her. But claiming her son's share? She'd fight tooth and nail to get *that*.

Yes, she'd make a name for herself, all right.

The maids moved around her, still giggling and chatting away. Her left hand was lifted to begin a massage, and they all stared down at the elegant yellow diamond. They sighed theatrically and smiled, and she sighed theatrically and played along with their little game.

She'd promised herself that she wouldn't torment herself with wondering what a *real* proposal would be like. After sticking that dagger in her own heart and twisting it around a few times she had consigned it to the 'Don't go there' list for evermore.

She closed her eyes and let the maids finish their pampering while she got her head around the next thing on her agenda. What a morning it had been so far—and it wasn't even ten a.m.

She'd cut Mariella off at the pass by phoning her at seven with the news. Making her the first to know and involving her in some of the planning was a shortcut to gaining her loyalty, but Salvatore wasn't going to be quite so easy to win over. He'd already made it plain that any half-sister was one too many.

Well, too bad. Nobody could change the past. All they could do was make the best out of the future. And, since they were going to be working together, she was going to give this meeting her best shot.

No matter how it went, she'd already arranged for a legal team to look after her affairs.

Suddenly the maids stopped chattering. The house seemed to pause. Doors sounded and voices rose.

They were here.

She felt her heart pound and all her muscles tense. The maid let go of her hand gently, and when she opened her eyes they were both scuttling off down the hallway.

Slowly her breathing settled. She scraped back the chair and focused once more on the room around her.

There was the bed she'd slept in just before she'd been asked to leave the island. There was the simple, beech chair where the red dress had been draped and the painful shoes had been dropped. On the bedside table was the lamp, now unlit, and the photograph of people she now knew to be Raffa's mother and father. Along the hallway she could hear the rumble of male voices—just like that night.

She stood up, dropped her shoulders and smoothed her dress. She touched a hand to her hair, then her bump and fleetingly twisted her diamond ring around her finger. This time she wasn't going to run into an ambush.

Along the passageway she went, her clicking heels announcing her arrival. They were both standing—Raffa close to Aphrodite's Pool and Salvatore leaning moodily against the wall.

'Hello, Salvatore,' she said, walking right up to him, hand outstretched, with a smile as broad as she could muster on her face. 'It's lovely to meet you properly at last.'

He turned. His face formed something that she assumed he thought was a smile.

'Coral. Welcome back to Hydros.'

'Lovely to be here, thank you. Did you have a good flight from Sydney?'

He narrowed his eyes and then he swung round.

'I can't do this, Raffa. I'm not going to pretend that this is right. This isn't what Papa would have wanted.'

Raffa stepped up. 'None of us know what Giancarlo really wanted. We don't know what it was like for him to know he had another child and not be able to do the right thing by everybody. But we are going to put right what we can, Salvatore. In the only way possible.'

He walked forward as he spoke, one step at a time, and each word was fearsome and forceful.

Coral's mouthful of retort was held in check for a moment.

'You're not being true to his memory, Raffa! You're just being blinded by this because she's dangling the carrot of your own little family right in front of your eyes. It's all a trap—to make me look bad and her look good. Don't you see?'

'You've done a wonderful job of looking bad without anyone's help,' Coral sliced in. 'I thought you would have the good grace to apologise for what you did, but I can see that I was hoping for too much.'

'Salvatore, I warned you not to cross the line—' said Raffa.

'Raffa, I can handle this. He has to hear it from me!' Coral interrupted.

But Salvatore ignored her, rounding on Raffa as if he was the only one in the room.

'*She's* the one to blame. We were fine before she lied her way onto the island. I know I've been difficult, but do you blame me? You *know* how hard it's been for me, Raffa!'

'We've never been "fine". I warned you, Salvatore. I told you where my loyalties lie. Now, give me a DNA sample and get out of here!'

Coral's hand flew to her mouth as Raffa lifted Salvatore by the collar and hauled him, ankles dragging on the ground, past the pool and out towards the terrace. Salvatore's limbs flailed as he tried to score punches. They reached the glass doors and she gasped as his body was flung against them. The chandelier's beads jittered. The dogs stood on alert by Raffa's feet, poised to attack.

Coral turned away as a sob rose in her throat. It was too hideous to watch. Her own flesh and blood and he hated her so much.

She began to retrace her steps, but in a heartbeat Raffa was at her side. She was in his arms, and he was holding her close. She clutched at his shirt and he smoothed his hand over her head.

'Shh…shh… It's OK. He's gone. He won't be back. I'm so sorry. I really thought he would be ready to meet you at least.'

'I don't understand—he wouldn't even give me a moment.'

'Don't criticise yourself. We tried. We did our best. And I've got the sample.'

He held out the phial and tucked it in his pocket.

'Why does he hate me so much? What did I ever do to him?'

'You did nothing. You have nothing to be ashamed of. It's always been this way. He hates me, too. Don't take it personally!' He let a tiny laugh lace his words and it eased her, just for a moment.

'If he hates me now, how is he going to feel when I file papers over the will?'

She felt Raffa's body tense.

He stepped back from her. 'What do you mean? You don't need to do that. I have more than enough. Maybe you don't know how much Romano is worth, but it's billions.'

'I can't leave it. You told me that in another month the whole estate will be settled. This is the only chance I have of putting things right.'

'You've no idea what you're saying, Coral. There's no need for this. All it will do is completely ruin Argento while you both fight it out in the courts. Salvatore will never surrender anything to you without a fight. You know that!'

He walked away to the window. She'd never seen him so angry. His shoulders were tense and his mouth was tense. His eyes blazed like lit gas. But she wasn't going to let herself be cowed by his anger.

'I've spent my whole life wondering who my father was, comparing myself to everyone else and coming off worst every time. Thinking I didn't deserve any happiness because I wasn't good enough. And now I find out what he was really like and—guess what? Turns out I'm not so bad after all. But Salvatore getting it all? I don't think so.'

'You do not need to do this. I don't want any harm to come to you.'

'What does *that* mean? You sound as if I should be worried. He doesn't frighten me. He's just a spoiled brat.'

'He's still your half-brother,' he said, his words laced with a trace of anger.

'*You're* the one who pointed out to me that I have responsibilities! I'm not doing this for *me*, Raffaele. I'm doing this for my baby and my mother—who is a shell of the woman she should have been.'

'Remember that your baby is *my* baby—and he doesn't need a penny of Di Visconti money. And your mother surely can't lay *all* the blame for her mental health at Giancarlo's door. Plenty of people have love affairs that don't work out, but it doesn't ruin their whole lives.'

'Yes, they have love affairs that don't work out—but they're not denied and ignored. I'm not saying that this is the only reason she's ill, but it didn't help. She got nothing from him. *Nothing!* Salvatore should have been on his knees begging forgiveness when he found out who I was, instead of having me thrown off this island.'

'Salvatore has his own demons.'

'Salvatore is an ass! And you've been covering it up for years—plastering over the cracks of this family because you feel that you might have caused some of them.'

His eyes blazed. Colour sprang high on his cheeks.

'You don't know what you're talking about.'

'Yes, I do. You just can't accept that someone can see through all the smoke and mirrors. The amazing Di Viscontis. It's all rubbish—the whole family is fake. The doting husband who has an affair, the amazingly successful son who is actually an incompetent fool. And you're so paranoid about anyone finding out that you cover it up!'

Suddenly another grotesque thought loomed in her mind. Was this marriage just another huge public relations manoeuvre?

'Is that what this wedding is really about? Oh, my God. *Please* don't tell me that this is just your attempt to keep the maverick illegitimate daughter under control. In case anyone finds out who I really am before you get a chance to write the press release!'

He walked away, running his hands through his hair. He raised his hands to the sky and muttered in Italian. Paced back towards her and held her by the arms.

'Is that what you think of me? You think I would marry you to prevent some unflattering news coming out? You're going to be my wife and you have learned nothing about me?'

She faltered and stared. Her eyes painted every line of his beautiful masculine face, every angle of his physique. She was falling deeper and deeper in love. There was no parachute, no safety net. If he was only doing this out of pride, she was going to crash and turn to dust.

'All I'm saying is that I don't want a marriage just to save face. It's wrong.'

She had to say it. She meant every word.

He slid his hand down to cup her face.

'It's not about saving face. It's because you're the best mother for our child.'

She shook her head. Tears sprang in her eyes.

'I don't need to be married to be a good mother. A husband is supposed to *love* his wife. Not see her as a glorified nanny. It's love that binds a family together. Not duty.

I was brought up in a tiny family, but there was so much love. You had all this—' She cast her arm out. 'But I truly don't know if you had any love. And if there's no love then there's nothing.'

Tears were thick and glassy in her eyes now. She had no more will to fight.

'What are you saying, Coral? That you don't want it now? You've changed your mind?'

She looked up at him. Her chin wobbled uncontrollably and her throat burned.

She shook her head. 'What is ahead for us, Raffaele?'

'Trust me! You *have* to trust me. I know what I'm doing. You're the right woman for me—I know that deep down.'

'I so want to believe that, Raffa,' she whispered. 'I really do.'

'Let me show you.'

He bent his head and kissed her.

The sobs that had gathered in her throat sighed away as his lips found hers.

'You're the most amazing woman.'

He held her face in his hands and she looked up into eyes etched with care. His took her hand, put it to his lips and kissed it. In that gesture, with the warmth and weight of the soft press of his lips on her skin, it was as if he'd found her Achilles' heel. As if she'd been pierced and the last of her fight had fizzled away.

'I've never met anyone like you. Your spirit, your integrity...'

And then he kissed her again. Gently, softly, and with such care. His lips pressed against hers, and when she began to respond he demanded more. Her body began to sing. He pulled her closer, but carefully. She felt each press of his hands, softly soothing her skin.

'Your beauty...'

He slid his hands down her arms and pulled her close. Then he wrapped his arms around her and she sighed into the embrace, feeling for the first time how it could be, how it *should* be. Mother, father and baby—one little unit. It felt so right, so incredibly perfect.

They stood, rocking slightly together, relearning each other's touch and scent, and her cares were soothed away with each passing second.

Suddenly the dogs started to bark. Cars rolled onto the driveway.

Her eyes flew open. 'My lawyers.'

'Send them away. You don't need them,' he said, kissing her again. 'We'll have more than enough. Don't start fighting Salvatore. It's not worth it.'

He started walking her back towards the bedroom, still kissing her. Her body ached for his hands, his lips.

'Raffa…' she breathed.

The dogs started to bark louder. She heard voices. Car doors closed and she looked through the windows at the small team of people, all dressed in black and grey, exiting the cars.

'I need to see them.'

'You don't need to do anything. I can handle everything for us.'

She shook her head. 'No,' she said. 'I told you. This is my condition. I want to make things right. My whole existence has been denied by the Di Viscontis and there's only a few weeks left to put it right. My son deserves *everything*. Not just half of everything.'

He stepped away and she sensed the coldness return. The shades went down over his eyes again.

'You're going to cause a war.'

'I'm going to stand up to Salvatore, if that's what you mean.'

'*I'll* deal with Salvatore.' His tone was sharp.

She fumed and breathed in deeply. '*I'll* deal with Salvatore!' she spat back. 'Just like I'll deal with all my own problems. If you can't handle that, then don't marry me!'

His eyes flashed and he took two more steps. Fury roared from his body, held back as the harbour wall held back the ocean. But she could see it—the points of colour on his cheeks, the grim set of his jaw and the proud lines of his chest.

'You have no idea what you're saying.'

'Yes, I do! I will not have the world filtered and sanitised because you think I can't cope with it. I will be your equal partner—in *everything*! Or I won't be your partner at all.'

'You've no idea what you're saying, Coral,' he repeated, more loudly.

'I'm saying what I feel is right, from the bottom of my heart. I want nothing more than justice for us all.'

'You want too much.'

His eyes were the clearest blue she had ever seen. His face, at that moment, had never looked more sorrowful, more beautiful. More utterly unattainable.

'Yes, I do. And I won't apologise for it.'

'Do you think going on the warpath is going to help our son?' He shook his head. 'A child needs a parent who is focused on *them*—not someone who is tearing up the world, trying to prove a point.'

'If I don't have the qualities you think I need to be your wife, then call it off.'

Her throat closed over the words. Her eyes burned with tears.

He stared at her, fierce and unforgiving. 'Oh, you're good, Coral. Very good. But be careful. If you push me too far…'

He shook his head and walked out, the dogs at his heels.

Coral walked to the pool and stared into the glassy surface.

The door banged closed.

CHAPTER THIRTEEN

THE VILLA MONTEROSSINI sat in the very heart of Rome, sur-rounded by topiary gardens to the front, sunken gardens to the rear and paved walkways that stretched in a criss-cross of lines across sweeping lawns. Screens of perfectly pruned trees and high stone walls kept it a secret from any passing traffic or perambulating tourists.

From the second floor, through vast floor-to-ceiling windows, Coral gazed out, her eyes landing on the foun-tain that bubbled and flowed, sprinkling each laughing cherub with delicate spray and sending rainbows in a haze all around.

What a beautiful day to be married, she thought, sip-ping the last of her tea and stepping back from the windows into the silk-carpeted dressing room. *What a beautiful, wretched day.*

The house was already buzzing with the barely con-tained wonder and delight of the elite teams who'd just arrived, laden with all the accoutrements of their trades and ready to work their magic in this, the grandest villa of its kind in Rome.

She could hear whispered gasps and muffled giggles from the hallway, as a team of people set up flowers and hung swathes of fabric. In the dressing room next door she could hear the hair and beauty team relaxing and joking between themselves, telling stories about who'd had too much to drink in the hotel the night before. Along the hallway came the high shrill tones of the housekeeper, slicing the air with instructions in very terse Italian.

She walked to the sideboard, ready to replace her cup and saucer on the gilt tray, and a maid came up immediately, ready to refill it. She smiled and waved her away.

It was impossible to want for anything in this house. In the three days since she'd arrived the staff had anticipated her every wish. There were fresh flowers in every room, scented oils in her bath and every tasty morsel imaginable to tempt her. They flattered her and spoiled her rotten.

Everyone was going out of their way to make her feel at home. Everyone except the *signor* himself.

From the moment she'd defied him and met with her lawyers he had closed down and headed off to Shanghai. He'd spoken on the phone to her each evening in quick, monosyllabic sentences, checking firstly her health, then her movements that day, and finally any comments she might have about the baby.

He'd told her the positive result of the second DNA test as if it was yesterday's weather forecast. And she had responded just as matter-of-factly.

He had never asked how she'd got on with the lawyers and she had never offered him any information. She'd kept back the fact that they'd told her she had a very good case.

They'd talked her through the whole process—what could go well and what might not. She'd seen the accounts, the years of work that had gone into building the cruise line from a tiny fleet to an international behemoth.

In recent years its growth had doubled and doubled again. Everyone acknowledged that Raffa was behind it, and yet he took nothing from the business—not even a director's salary. And so the seeds of doubt that she should claim any of it had been sown.

Still, papers had been drawn up in readiness for her final decision. And soon she would give it—soon. As soon as the wedding was over.

Finally the day had come.

Her mother would be arriving within the hour, following the most difficult phone call of her life. She walked to the sofa and sat down heavily, thinking of her mother's imminent arrival. She had expected tears and grief, but it seemed that a wedding could solve almost everyone's worries.

Lynda had expressed concern for Coral, and sought reassurances that she knew what she was doing. Then, just as she had been about to hang up, grateful that the whole ordeal was out in the open, she'd asked that final gut-wrenching question.

'Do you love him?'

Her mouth had formed the word before her mind had had a chance to catch up.

'Yes,' she'd blurted, tears springing in her eyes.

'Well, that's all that matters, then.'

But I don't think he loves me back, she'd whispered to herself.

She couldn't tell her mother that.

She could barely admit it to herself.

So Lynda Dahl would be walking with a spring in her step for the first time in twenty-five years. And Coral would be dragging her satin-covered heels all the way to the altar.

'Are you ready to bathe?' a maid asked, her face beaming with undisguised joy. 'There are less than three hours before the wedding starts!'

Coral smiled and stood up slowly.

'First I must check in with Chef about the food, and make sure everyone has everything they need.'

The maid laughed. 'It's all taken care of. Come. Anyone would think you didn't want to get married!'

The maid pulled at her hands gently and she went along with her through the hallway, where the tables were now overflowing with huge arrangements of white roses, gardenias and lilies. The staircase that swept down to the ground floor was dotted with simple, voluminous white satin bows, and all along the passageway to the glass-walled garden room ivy and roses trailed prettily above elegant arrangements of candles.

In less than three hours those seats would be filled with the great and the good of international high society—and a scattering of London artists.

She and Raffaele would stand before God and make promises and she would mean every word—because she knew now that nothing would be the same again. No man could fill every pore of her being with love the way this man did. He would slip a ring on her finger and they would kiss and it would all be one big loveless transaction.

She walked into the master bedroom where the four-poster bed was draped in the finest ivory silk. She walked past the mannequin that held her dress and wished that she were as wooden. She walked past the beauticians, who beamed as they arranged their make-up boxes, brushes and pots into a garish rainbow.

On she went into the bathroom. Through the steam she saw the huge egg-shaped bath on gilt feet, two-thirds full of water and slick with scented oil that she knew would be absolutely perfect.

Everything in her world was absolutely perfect. Almost.

She slipped her feet out of her slippers, stood beside the bath and allowed herself to be disrobed.

When she stepped out of the bath she'd be ready to become a wife. A wife to Raffaele, the most eligible man in the media world. The most eligible man in Italy. Handsome, enigmatic and wealthy beyond her wildest dreams. A man of immense honour and integrity. A man who would sacrifice his own happiness for the sake of others. A man whose nearness set her body ablaze, whose lips could caress her into a frenzy of longing. A man whose mind and heart she loved dearly.

She stepped in the water and sank down into its warmth. Sank down miserably into her fate.

Because no matter how they dressed her up, and dressed up this house, no matter how happy her mother was and how much her baby needed a father, marrying a man who did not love her back was just not right.

How could she live with herself?

She sat there, refusing offers of help until the water began to get chilly. Her breasts were larger than ever and her belly huge. She ran her hands over her skin, touching the shape of her child, feeling for his little foot or elbow, sighing her love through her tears and wishing that the love she could give him would be enough.

But it wouldn't.

Finally the staff began to muster like a pack of anxious puppies. She couldn't put it off any longer. She must get out of the bath and get dressed.

They were prattling on in Italian—she was beginning to pick up more every day—and then she heard a new voice, a different tone. The housekeeper.

The *signor* still wasn't here. He might not be coming. Should they interrupt the *signorina*?

What if he didn't come? She'd *known* it was too good to be true. What if he didn't want to go ahead with it? What if….

Coral's eyes flew open. She pulled herself up to her feet. The water sloshed around her and over the sides of the bath, landing on the tiled floor in one big splash. The door burst open and the maids appeared, looking shocked.

'*Di cosa stai parlando*? *Dov'e*?' Coral demanded. 'What do you mean, he might not be coming? Where is he? How dare you stand out there gossiping?'

The maids rushed forward, crying out apologies and trying to wrap her up in towels.

'Please, *signora*, please get ready. It's just silly gossip. It means nothing. You must get dressed. You're so cold. Please.'

They bustled her through the bathroom and into the dressing room, which had miraculously been cleared of staff. They sat her on the bed like a marionette and she let them dry her.

'But why isn't he here? What has happened?'

She stared around the room. Everything was set out for the preparation of the bride. Everything in its place, waiting to be painted or curled or puffed into life. Waiting for the moment she would meet her groom.

But there was no groom.

'What will I do if he doesn't come?'

She was thinking aloud, mumbling her words, struggling to come to terms with all that was unravelling around her.

'Of course he'll come. He's always so busy. He must have so much to do before he comes for you. You're so lovely, *signorina*. He must love you so very much. You and the little *bambino*.'

They smoothed lotions on her legs and arms, massaging her gently, chattering away. But she saw them exchanging glances nervously. Anxiously preparing her for a wedding that might not take place.

They led her over to a leather chair. Her hair was brushed and sprayed and set in huge rollers. The friendly chatter started up again, gentle jokes between them all, but this time it sounded false and tinny.

She asked for her phone.

There were no messages or calls.

She asked who had arrived at the house. Her mother was approaching by car. Her flight had landed some twenty minutes ago. But there was still no sign of Raffaele.

Her eyes crushed closed. What was she to say to everyone? The guests…? Her mother…?

Carefully, they began to apply her make-up. Her skin was unblemished—radiant, she was told. Never had they seen such a perfect bride. More beautiful than any film star, more natural than any model, she was going to melt the *signor*'s heart.

But still he did not come.

Maybe he had changed his mind. He had thought her selfish and greedy for wanting to claim her inheritance. Perhaps he had decided she was too foolhardy to be trusted as his wife.

Her mind ran wild with scenarios.

Or had he finally realised that marrying without love was wrong?

She asked for her phone again. Still no messages.

She sent the staff away and called him.

Straight to voicemail. That had never, *ever* happened before.

Since the moment he had appeared back in her life, the strong, silent mountain of his presence had been right there. She had battled against it but it had stayed there, strong and sure. The thought that she might not have it there any longer chilled her to the bone.

As if a sickness had come over her she stood up, felt

her brow and looked around. She had to get away—escape from this panic, this grief, the hideous public catastrophe that lay ahead.

She stepped to the door.

And looked up into his face.

There he was.

'Raffa!' she cried. 'Where have you been? What's—?'

His face was grim and set in harsh, cold lines. His eyes were cloaked with pain.

He stepped inside and closed the door.

She stopped there, a foot away from him, held back by the chill that seeped out of him like the darkest, coldest, harshest frost.

'We need to talk,' he said.

And her heart sank through the floor.

CHAPTER FOURTEEN

HE COULDN'T REMEMBER when he had first learned how important it was to control fear. And how easy it was. All you had to do was recognise it and then calmly and methodically think through all the different worst-case scenarios. Then deal with them one by one. It worked every time.

It had to have started the day of the crash, when he had been waiting to be taken home from school for Christmas. He'd never felt such excitement, such longing to see his parents after the long, lonely weeks as a boarder. Then the police had come. He had known even before Matron had told him. He had seen the fear in her eyes.

He'd never forgotten that fear. Nothing could ever be that bad again.

He could never get rid of fear entirely, but he could stop his anxiety taking on a life of its own by working harder than anyone, by being indispensable—by marrying Coral.

No. The time had come to stop feeding his paranoia. To stop the disaster movie that ran in his head on a loop. Marriage wouldn't keep any of them safe—it would just reassure him that he had covered more bases.

'There won't be a wedding, Coral,' he said, quietly and calmly.

Colour drained from her face. Her hand flew to her

belly and that gesture twisted the knife that was stuck in his heart even more deeply.

'Wh—why? What's happened?'

A white satin robe enveloped her beautiful body...a white scarf was wrapped around her hair. She looked more lovely than ever.

'Did *he* tell you to do this? Salvatore? Is he behind this?'

'What? No. Salvatore is... Salvatore is not my concern any more.'

'Why are you doing this, Raffa? Why now, when everyone is downstairs waiting? When I am ready to step into my dress? What has happened to make you change your mind?'

Tears were forming in her eyes. She wiped them away and he watched as a trail of brown shadow was smeared on her cheekbone.

'I can't force something because it's how I think it should be.'

'Is it because I said I wanted my inheritance? Is that it? Surely you can see that I need to have an identity other than being someone's wife or someone's mother? *I* need to provide for the baby too.'

Her chin wobbled as she spoke. Her voice wavered.

He looked away. 'Of course I do. I truly do. And I accept that. But it was wrong of me to think that we had to marry for us to parent our child. I know you'll be a brilliant mother to him.'

'So we won't live together either?'

He walked around the room, picking up the bride-to-be artefacts. So much feminine clutter. The whole house was bedecked and throbbing with excitement. Very important people from all over the world were here to honour this extraordinary event. Everyone's head had turned as he'd careered into the driveway and raced up the stairs.

'We don't have to do anything we don't want to. We can draw up our own arrangement or have the legal sharks cut it up for us. It's up to you.'

'But what about our plans? Our child needs us both! That was what you said.'

He was standing now, right beside her wedding dress. He lifted his fingers to touch the delicate lace sheath. She would have looked so lovely. A huge ivory ribbon was tied just under the bust and trailed down the sides to the knee-length hem. He lifted it up, letting it slip through his fingers.

'We can make new plans. I've already siphoned off MacIver. It's there if you want it. You could create something amazing and it would be all yours. I've no influence with Argento. I'm sorry if boats float your boat, so to speak, but I really have done with that now. The lawyers are untying me as we speak.'

He heard her sob. He didn't want to look round. He walked to the window and addressed the stupid little topiary hedges that he'd hated ever since he was a child.

'I know you think I'm interfering, but I'd do anything for you not to be involved in any way with Salvatore—even if you're fighting him. He's poisonous. You deserve better. And, don't ask me why, but I really want you to take my *other* baby. Take MacIver. Make it work. That's what you really want, isn't it, Coral? To make your mark on the world?'

He took her silence for confirmation. Every second was like another year of a jail term.

'I'll deal with the guests. You don't need to face anyone. I'll leave you here in Rome—you can have the house. I'll take you to London, or back to Hydros. Tell me what you want, Coral, and I'll make it happen for you. I promise you.'

'No, you won't you—you...*bastard*! You will not do this to me!'

He froze. 'What did you say?'

She was halfway across the floor. She was untying the robe and throwing it down on the ground. Underneath she wore exquisite lingerie that hugged her wonderful curves, and stockings on her long, elegant legs.

'You will *not* do this to me!'

She grabbed the wedding dress from the wooden mannequin and unzipped it. The mannequin wobbled back and forth as if in shock. She stepped into the dress, never taking her eyes off his.

'*You* made love to me, Raffaele Rossini! *You* made me pregnant. Then you threw me out, and then wouldn't let me out of your sight until you were sure I wasn't a liar! And then you made me fall in love with you. You utter...'

The dress was on. The ribbon lay limp down one side. She tugged at the zip, staring at him as if she wanted to brand him with her eyes.

'What did you say?' he breathed.

'You heard!' she said.

He paced towards her.

He put his hand up to silence her.

'What. Did. You. Say?'

He reached her. She was still struggling with the dress, twisting her arms up over her shoulders and pulling at the zip.

He grabbed her by the wrists. 'What did you say, dammit?'

'You *will* marry me if it's the last thing you do,' she breathed, staring up at him through the most blurry, beautiful eyes he had ever seen.

'Oh, I will, will I?' he asked, not moving a muscle.

Her eyes blinked. Her shoulders sank. Her lips fell open and she let her head fall down, just for a moment.

But then she looked up and into his eyes, and he felt

something shift in his heart. Something shifted and settled and he knew then that he was going to be with this woman for the rest of his life.

'You love me, don't you?' he said.

She looked him right in the eye. And then she nodded. 'Yes. Yes, I do.'

He gathered her into his arms. This wild, wanton woman who was his…his everything. He held her closer than close. He cradled her and rocked her and breathed his love.

'You do. And I love you, too.'

She grabbed his shirt, handfuls of it, and laid her head on his chest.

'You've got a funny way of showing it.'

He held her closer still. He wouldn't let her go.

'I've never shown it to anyone before. You'll need to help me practise.'

She nodded, but still she didn't move. She was happy in his arms. He could feel it. This was love. Unconditional. Uncontracted. *Real.*

He fell to his knees.

'Marry me, Coral. Make me the happiest man alive. Promise you'll never change, never do what you're told, never shut up and sit quietly or behave. Promise that you'll win over the media world as you've won *me* over.'

'Oh, Raffaele!'

'I know in my heart that my mother and father would have loved you.'

She flung her arms around his neck. Their mouths met and they kissed and he felt her love.

'I've wanted you so much, Coral. From the moment—'

'The moment you saw me coming off the jet. I know. You told me.'

He smiled. She was *his* woman. There was no other for him but her.

'After you tried to hide your pregnancy I was so angry with you for thinking I wouldn't look after you.'

'I would never have done that if you hadn't thrown me out.'

'That's my only regret. It was awful. But when you pulled off that dress and threw it at me I knew I was going to marry you.'

At that, she pulled back. She looked up. Her eyes were sooty and tear-stained, but she glowed like a sunrise in summer.

'Did you really?'

He pulled her back into the warmth of his embrace and laid his chin on her head.

'I knew I wanted to chase you down and never let you go.'

'Never let me go?' she repeated.

They stood locked together as the minutes ticked by, three becoming one.

'Do you think they're all still here?'

'I think so.'

'Do you think we should go down and see?'

'We're going to have to make this legal some time.'

'Do you think we'll hit the headlines?'

'There's every chance. There are two news anchors and about a dozen of the world's top journalists down there.'

'Maybe we should give them a story.'

'I think they've got all the story they need. You're the most unconventional, adorable bride in history.'

'No best man, no bridesmaids, no one giving me away. Just the three of us.'

Coral gazed up into the face of the man she loved.

He tucked a stray lock of hair behind her ear. 'Your mother did a wonderful job raising you, Coral.'

She bit her lip and he could see she was holding back

more tears. She nodded, held herself in check, and when she opened her eyes again the love was shining forth.

'That was the right thing to say, Raffa. She did. She was a wonderful mother and—'

'And so will you be, my darling. So will you.'

EPILOGUE

'HAVE YOU HEARD the latest rumour?' Coral asked as she buttered a piece of toast and cut it into quarters. She put it on Matteo's tray and watched while his chubby fingers closed around a piece.

'Gossip doesn't interest me at any time of the day, but I'm particularly not keen to hear it until I've had at least three coffees. As you well know, my darling.'

'Hmm, yes…but this you'll want to hear.'

Raffaele made a dismissive sound and carried on reading his newspaper.

'Daddy's grumpy,' she said, giving Matteo a huge smile.

'Daddy gwump!' Matteo said, beaming back, his cherubic cheeks smeared with butter and crumbs.

'Stop teaching him bad words,' said Raffaele. 'I am *not* grumpy. I'm just a little more tired than usual this morning.'

Coral laughed, and Matteo laughed with her.

'Did you make Daddy tired, Matty? Did you play games and run along the beach all day long?'

She reached for her precious bundle and unclipped him from the safety harness in his high chair.

Raffaele put his paper down. 'Yes, he did. Even the dogs were exhausted.'

Coral clasped Matteo tightly, loving the sensation of

the tiny bones in his warm, strong little body. In a second he had a handful of her hair, rolling it round in his sticky little fingers.

'He loves your hair as much as I do.'

'Almost!' She laughed, untangling his fingers. 'So, what did you get up to yesterday?'

Raffaele stood up, putting his arms out for his boy. Coral slid Matteo across.

'All the favourites,' he said. 'As soon as you were in the air we were on the beach—were we not?' he said, jiggling Matty in his arms. 'Sandcastles. Paddling. Then we had a picnic lunch and then we did it all over again.'

'Get any work done?'

'Not a thing. When he slept, I did too. How about you? Did the shoot go to plan?'

Coral smiled, sat down and poured herself another cup of tea.

'It was fabulous, thanks.' She cradled the cup between her hands and blew away the steam. 'The location was absolutely perfect. We threw out all the ideas and just shot the Princess riding her horse as the sun came up.'

'Wasn't it couture?'

'Yes. Ball gowns—with a touch of Lady Godiva,' Coral said, laughing. 'It was so much fun.'

She put her cup down and looked up at her husband and child. They were both watching her carefully.

'What is it?' she said.

'Only love. That's all,' said Raffa. 'You've transformed MacIver, but you still want to get up to your armpits in pictures. It's lovely. It makes me so happy.'

'I couldn't have done it without you, darling.'

'I love my time at home with Matty. It's the best possible way to raise a child. I thank God every day that we are lucky enough to be able to do it.'

Coral nodded. 'Me too. I better call Mum later. Check how she's getting on with this new gallery. It seems to be going well.'

'I called her yesterday. She's fine.'

Coral smiled. He was so good, so attentive—to her and the baby and to her mother, too.

'You're really not interested in the rumour, then?'

Raffa had put Matty on the floor and was holding his hand as he toddled backwards and forwards.

'If it's another story about Salvatore trying to start another cruise company, I think I've heard them all.'

'No, we both know that his walking away from Argento with that enormous pay-off and then having to hand it straight over to Kyla was the best example of karma ever. She won't let him near a negotiating table again, that's for sure.'

Coral put down her napkin and pushed back her chair.

'I'm going to have to come right out with it then, am I?'

Raffa scooped Matty up into his arms, smiling at his squeals of delight.

'No,' he said, walking towards her.

With one arm he held Matty tight against his chest, and with the other he drew Coral in beside him, nestling the three of them together. He was beaming at her, his blue eyes sparkling like the sea in high summer.

'I already know the rumour. You're pregnant. I can see it in your eyes. They're dancing. Full of life. Just like the last time.'

She pulled back, astonished.

'You are, aren't you?'

'I can't hide a *thing* from you, can I?'

'Nothing. And this time I'm going to be here for you every step of the way.'

Raffa put Matty back in the high chair, strapped him in,

and while their infant son guzzled another piece of toast he took his wife in his arms and kissed her.

He kissed her with love, and Coral knew that no matter what happened they had each other. They would raise their family and grow old and grey together, growing happier by the day.

* * * * *

If you enjoyed
THE CONSEQUENCE SHE CANNOT DENY
why not explore these other stories
by Bella Frances?

THE ARGENTINIAN'S VIRGIN CONQUEST
THE ITALIAN'S VENGEFUL SEDUCTION
THE PLAYBOY OF ARGENTINA

Available now!